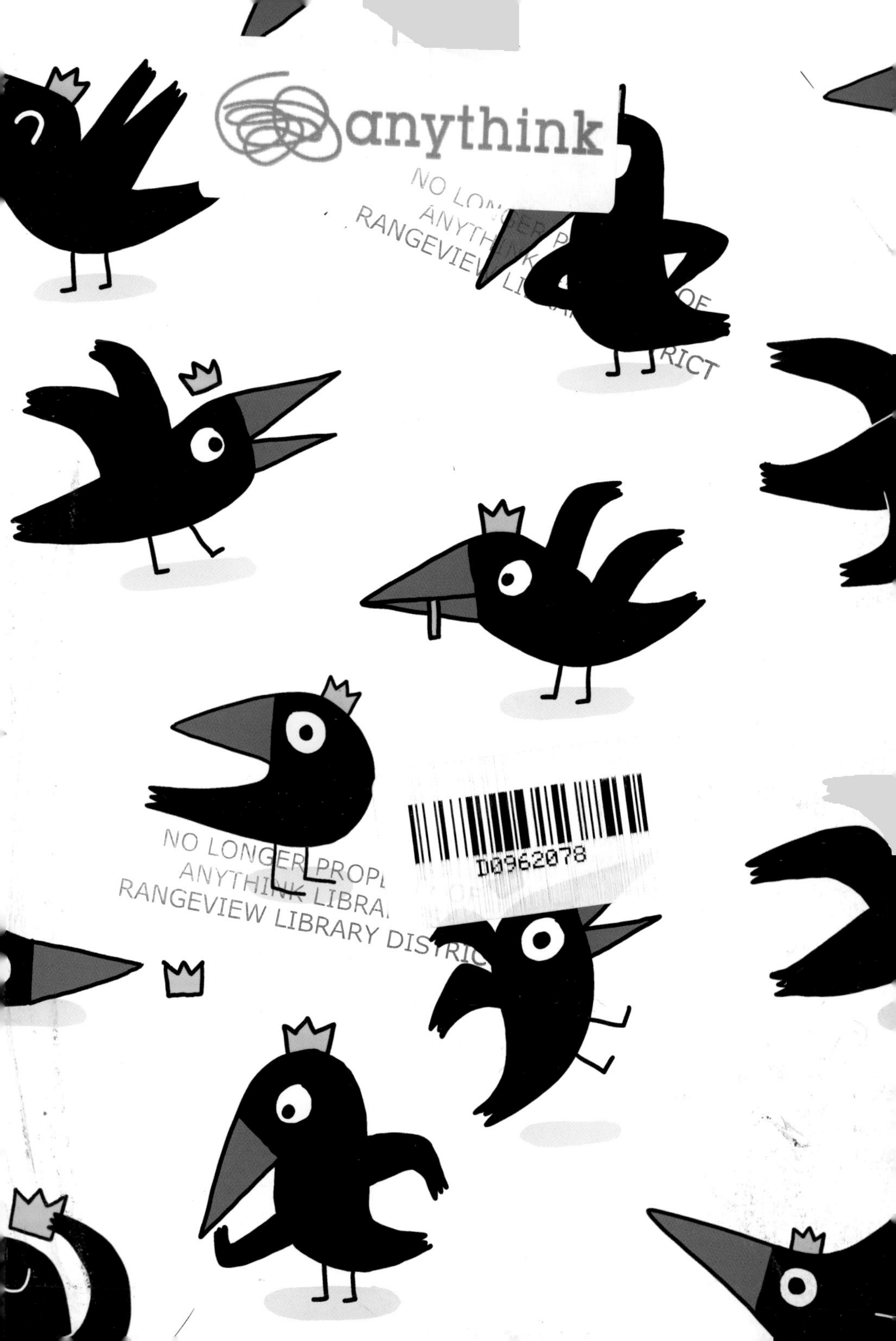

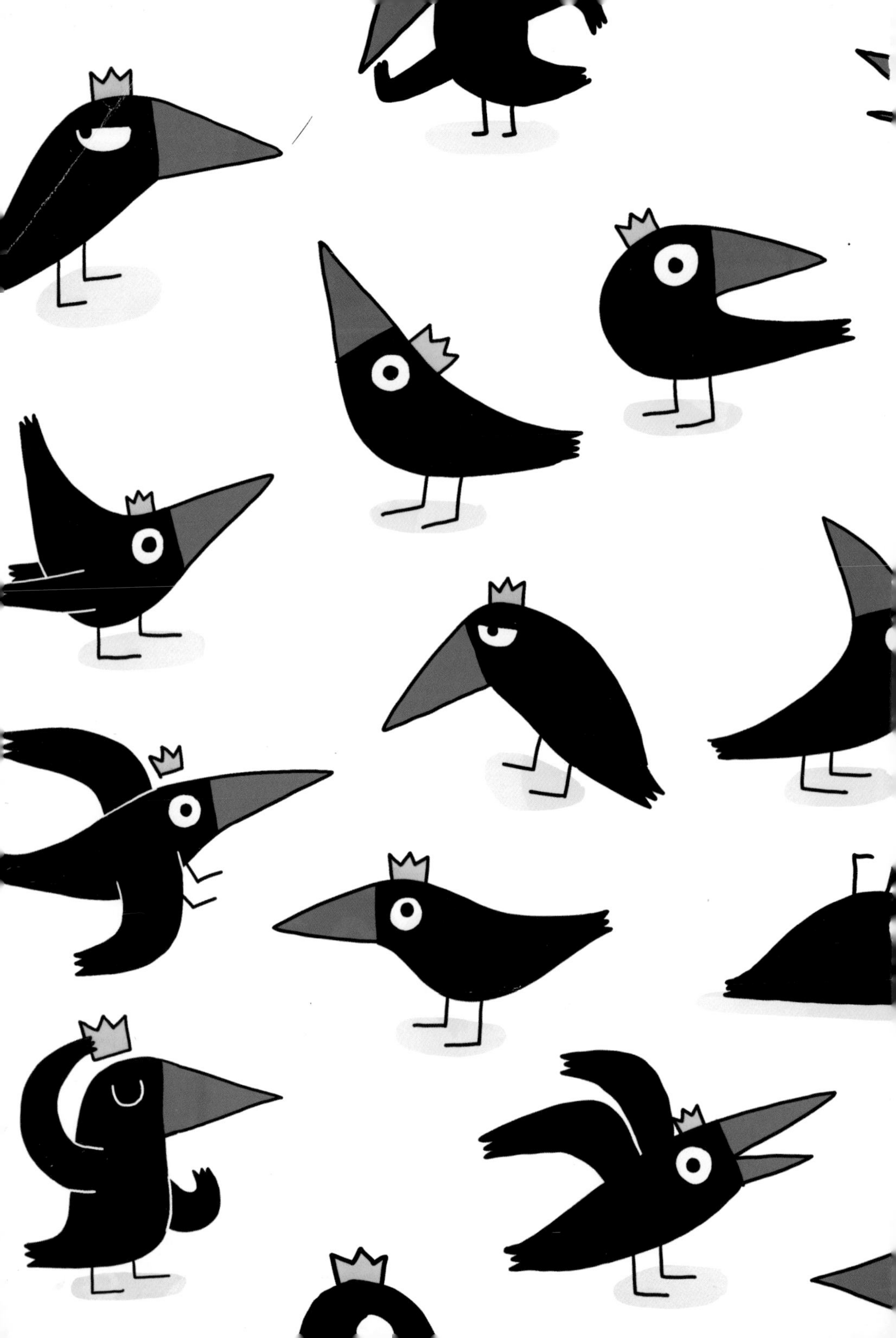

# ✮✮✮ ARLO & PIPS ✮✮✮

# KING OF THE BIRDS

## ELISE GRAVEL

HARPER
alley

*An Imprint of HarperCollinsPublishers*

HarperAlley is an imprint of HarperCollins Publishers.

Arlo & Pips: King of the Birds
Copyright © 2020 by Elise Gravel
All rights reserved. Manufactured in Slovenia.
No part of this book may be used or reproduced in any manner whatsoever without written permission except in the case
of brief quotations embodied in critical articles and reviews. For information address HarperCollins Children's Books, a
division of HarperCollins Publishers, 195 Broadway, New York, NY 10007.

www.harpercollinschildrens.com

ISBN 978-0-06-298221-6 (tr.) — 978-0-06-298222-3 (pbk.)

The artist used Photoshop to create the digital illustrations for this book.
Typography by Elise Gravel and Chrisila Maida
20 21 22 23 24 GPS 10 9 8 7 6 5 4 3 2 1

❖
First Edition

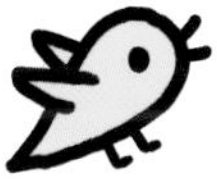

For Enzo,
who is almost an Arlo

On the highest mountains

and the greenest prairies,

in the biggest cities

and the deepest forests,

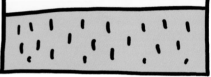

in the whole universe

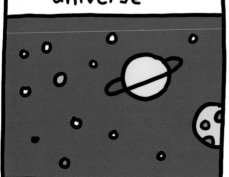

no bird
is greater
than . . .

4

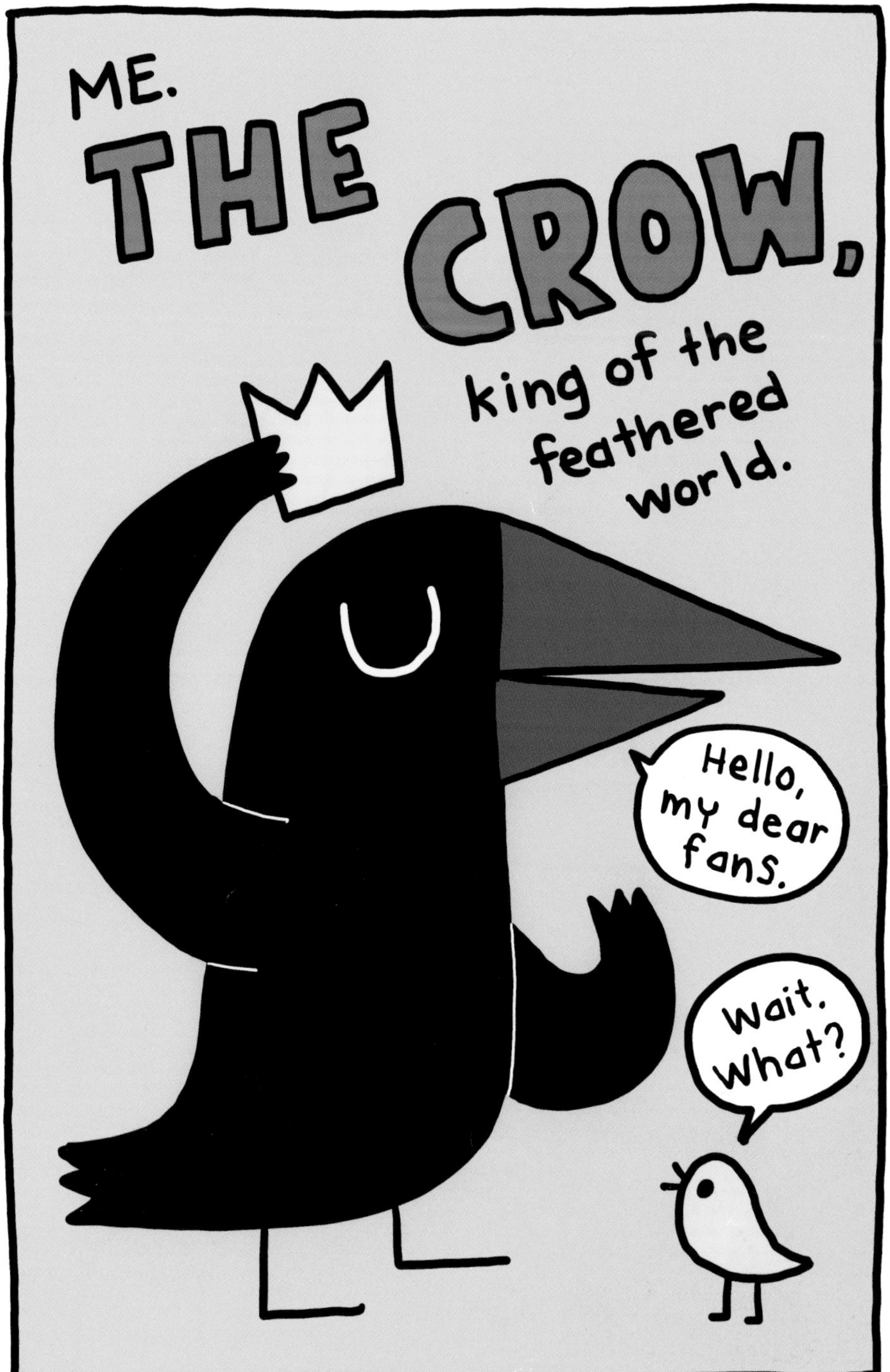
ME.
THE CROW,
king of the feathered world.
Hello, my dear fans.
Wait. What?

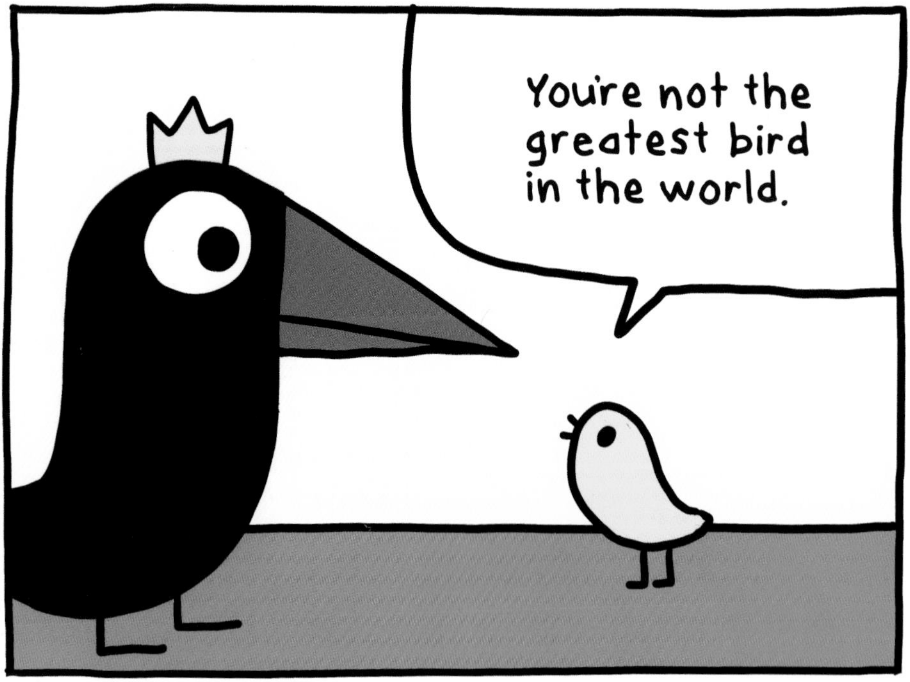
You're not the greatest bird in the world.

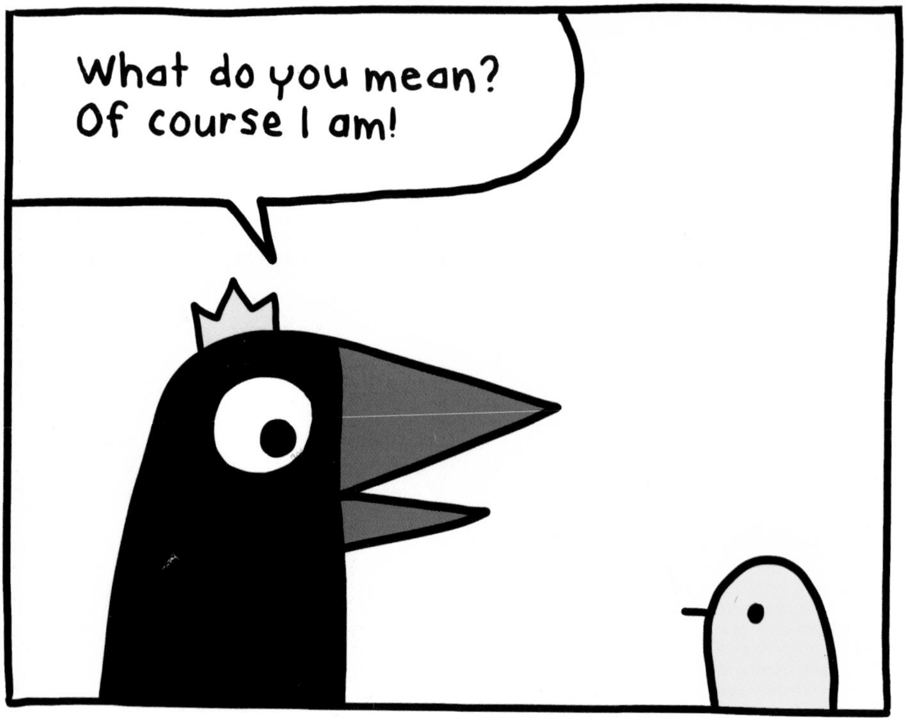
What do you mean? Of course I am!

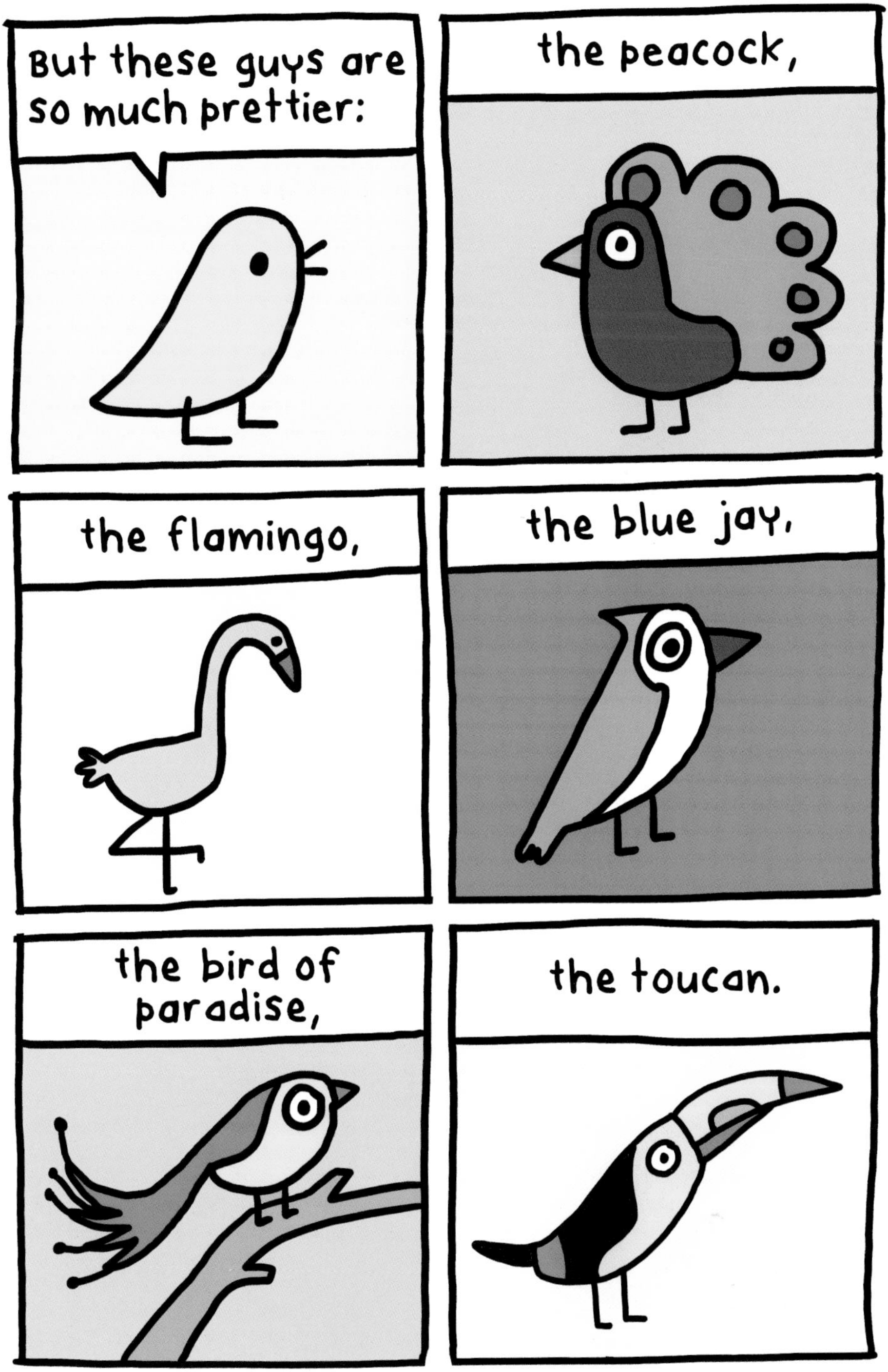
But these guys are so much prettier:
the peacock,
the flamingo,
the blue jay,
the bird of paradise,
the toucan.

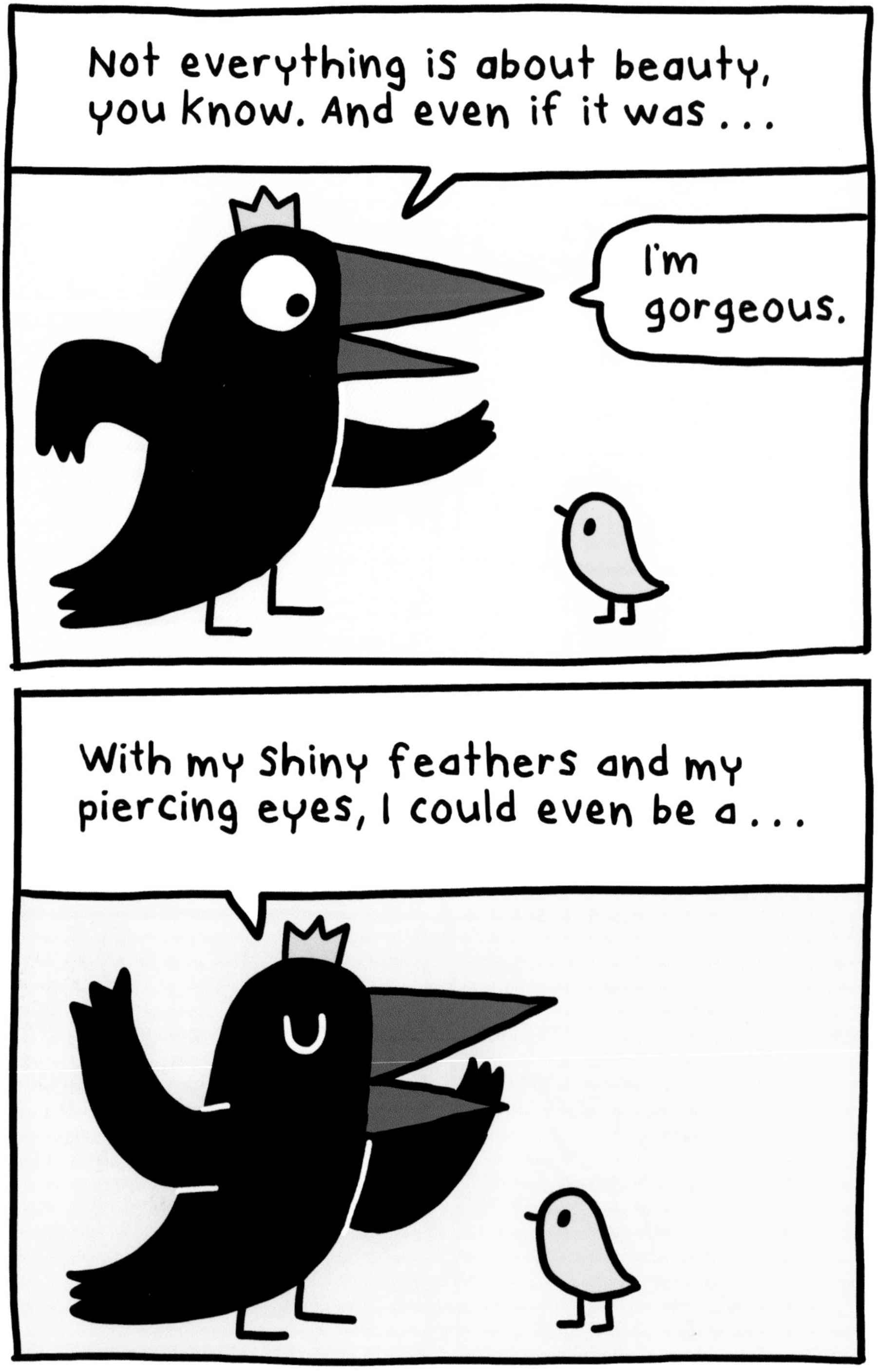
Not everything is about beauty, you know. And even if it was . . .
I'm gorgeous.
With my Shiny feathers and my piercing eyes, I could even be a . . .

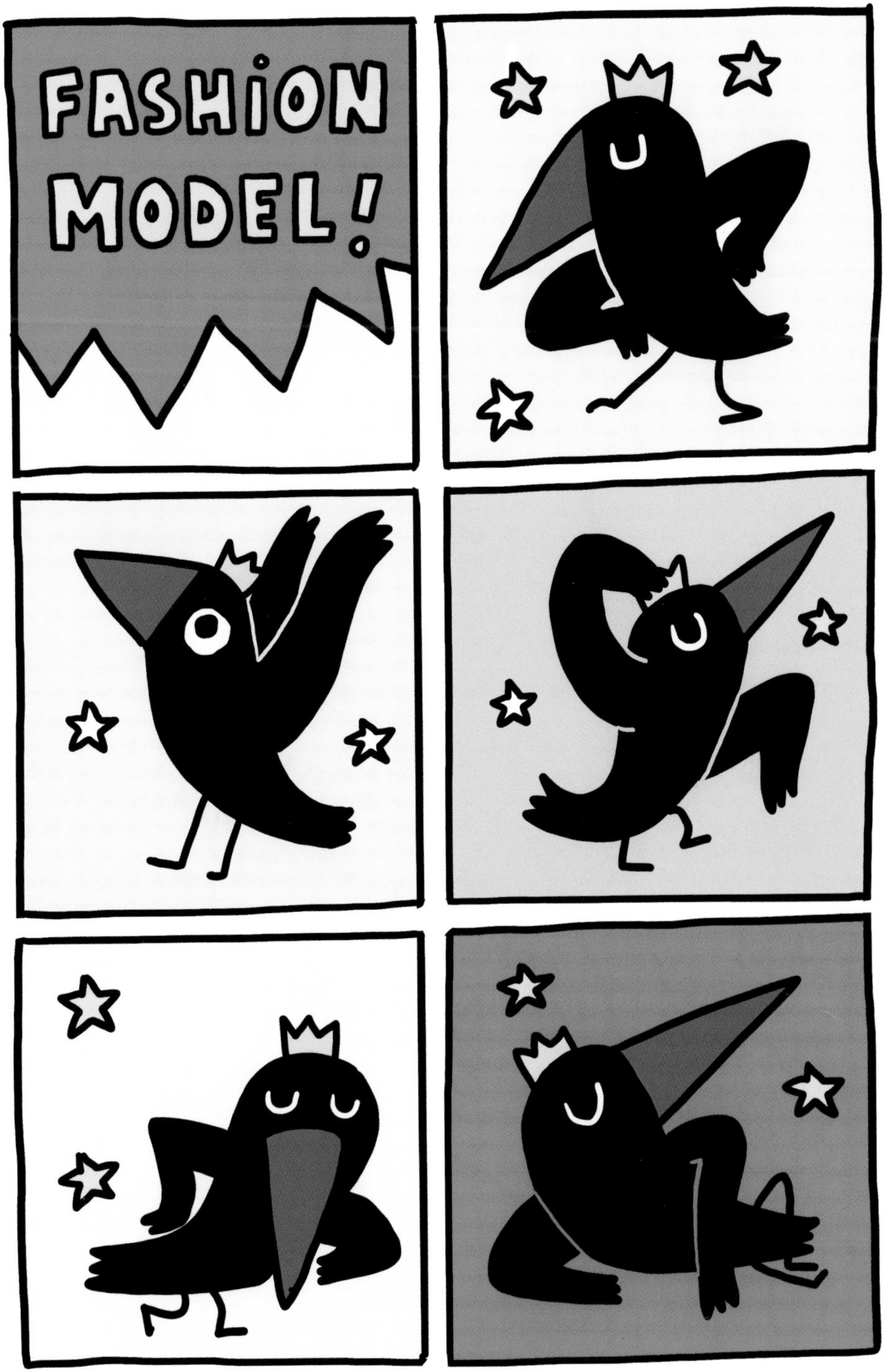
FASHION MODEL!

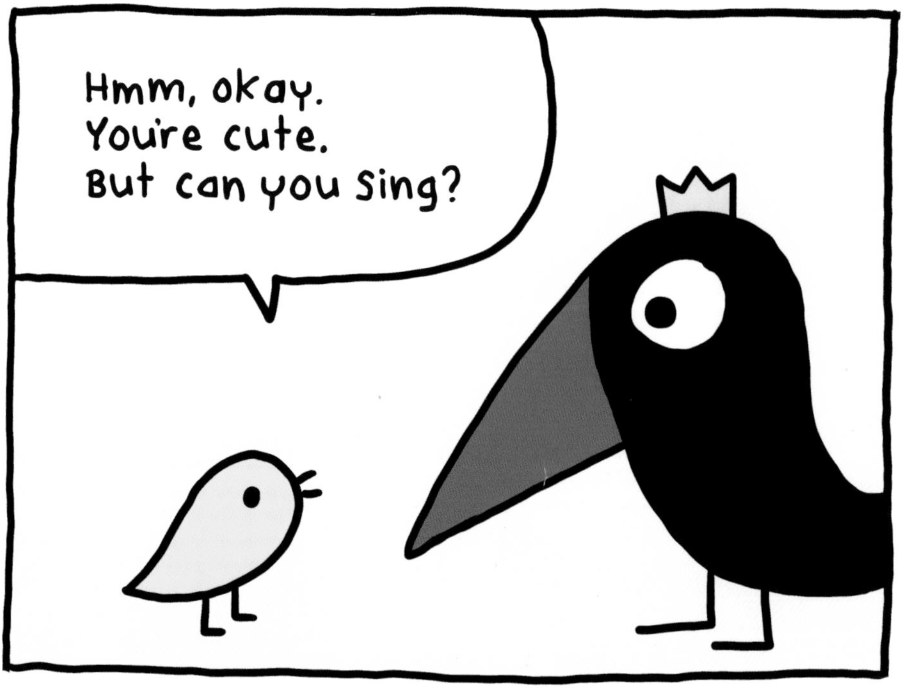
Hmm, okay.
You're cute.
But can you sing?

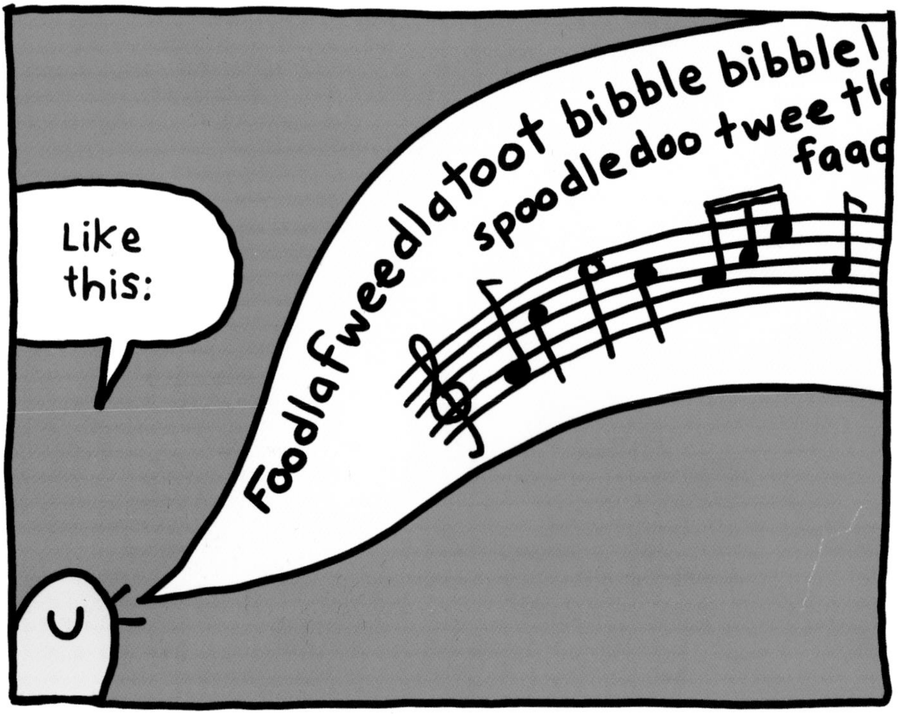
Like this:
Foodlafweedlatoot bibble bibblel
spoodledoo twee tl
faa

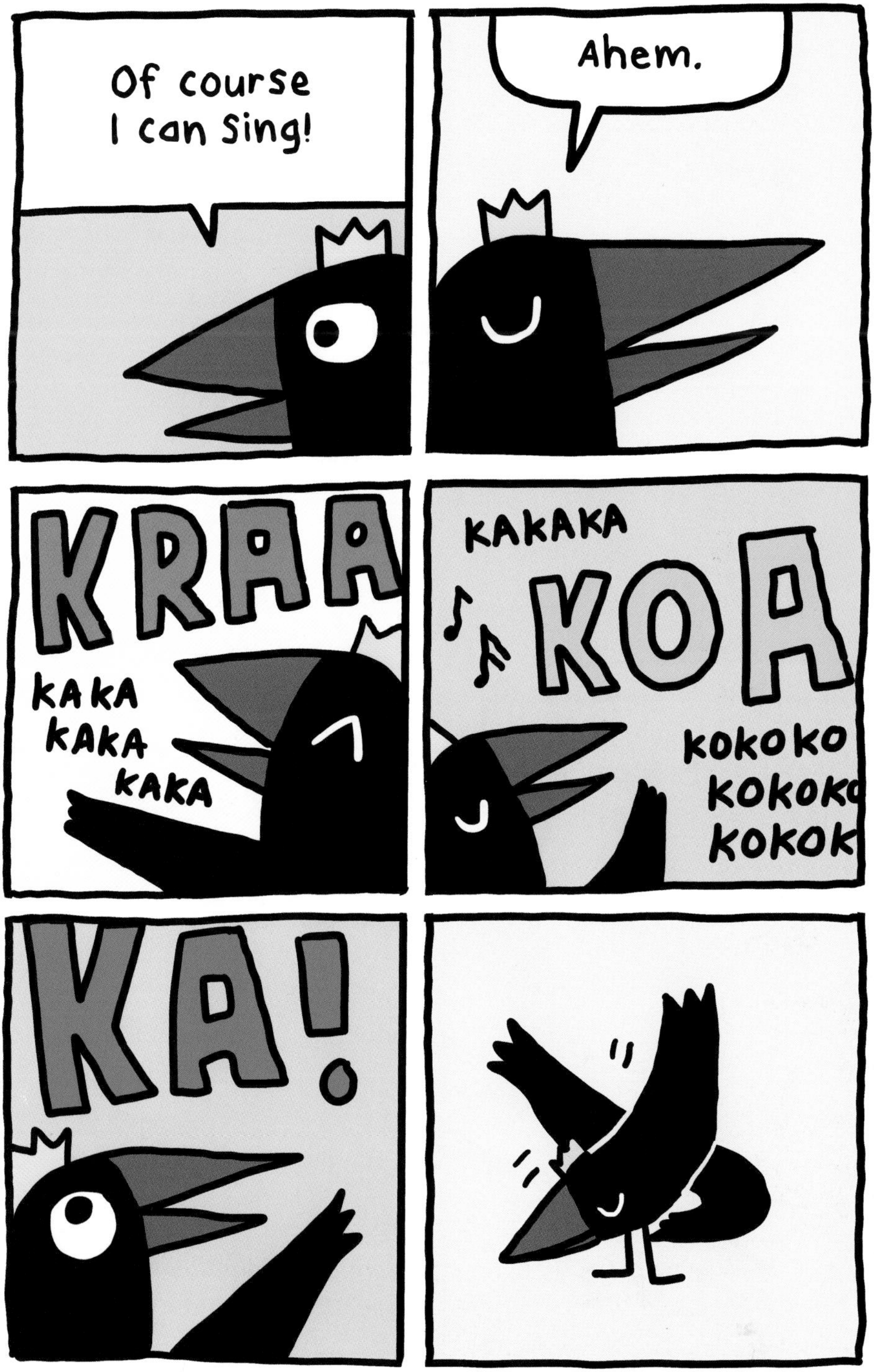
Of course I can sing!
Ahem.
KRAA
KAKA KAKA KAKA
KAKAKA
KOA
KOKOKO KOKOKO KOKOK
KA!

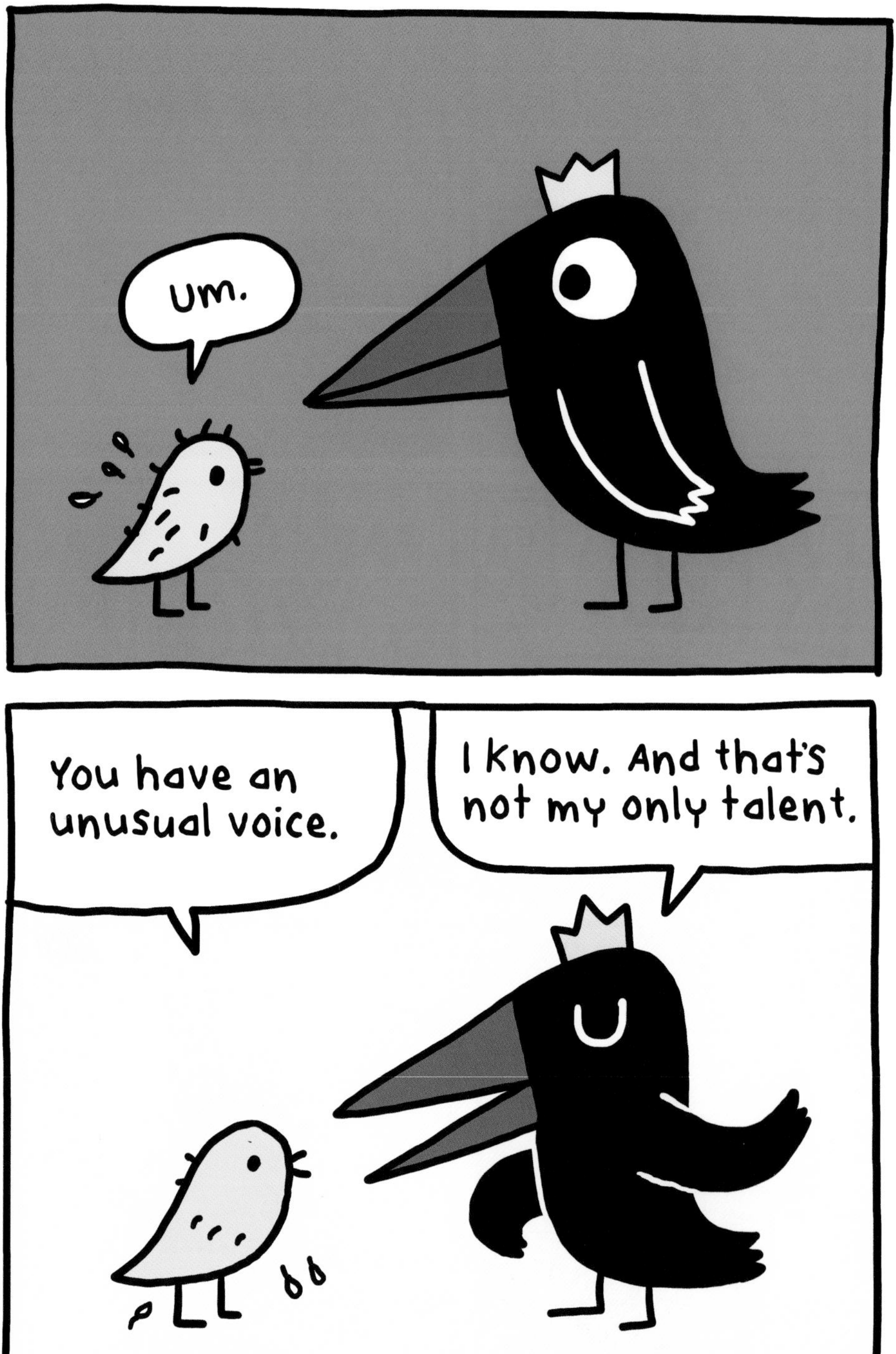
Um.
You have an unusual voice.
I know. And that's not my only talent.

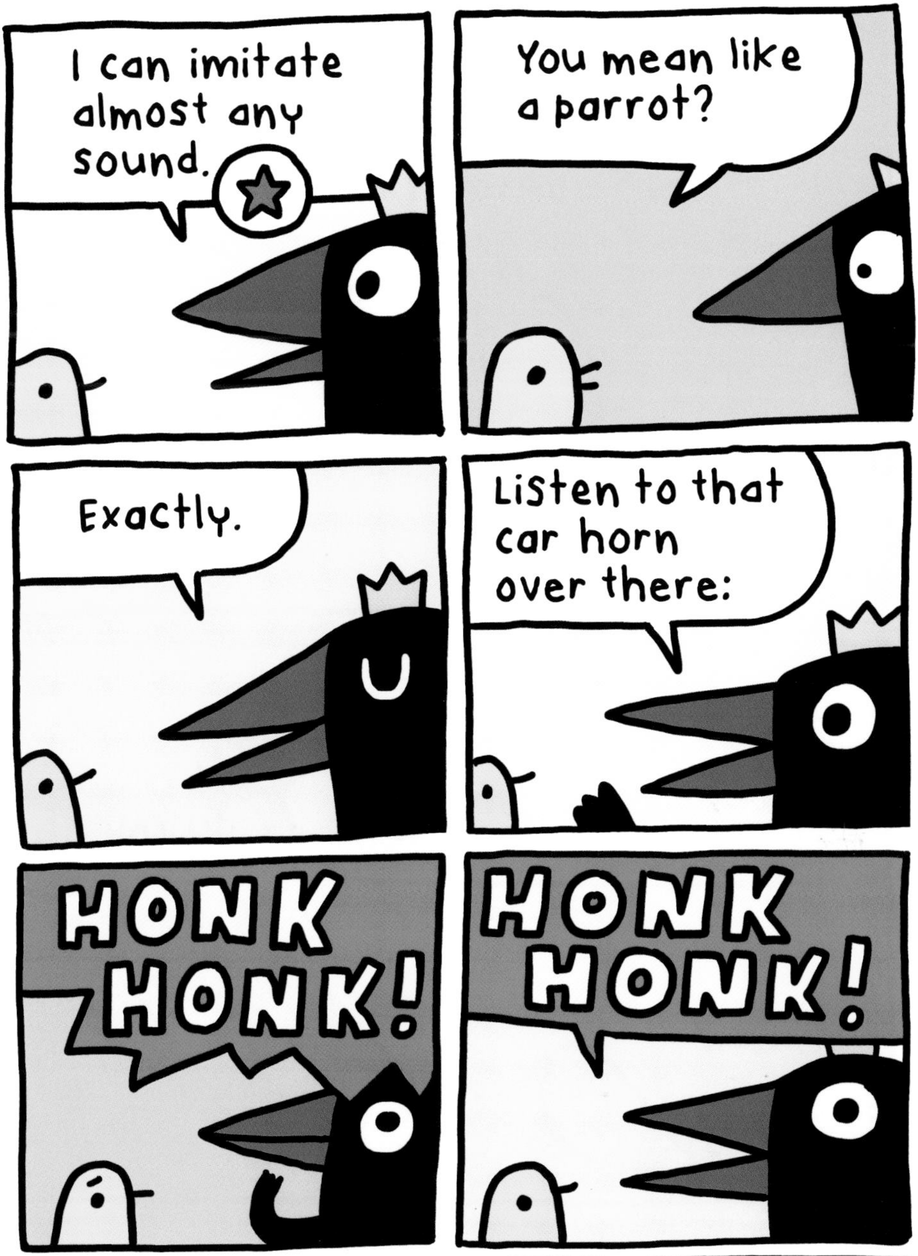
I can imitate almost any sound.
You mean like a parrot?
Exactly.
Listen to that car horn over there:
HONK HONK!
HONK HONK!

★ Crows are very good at imitating sounds, including human voices and words.

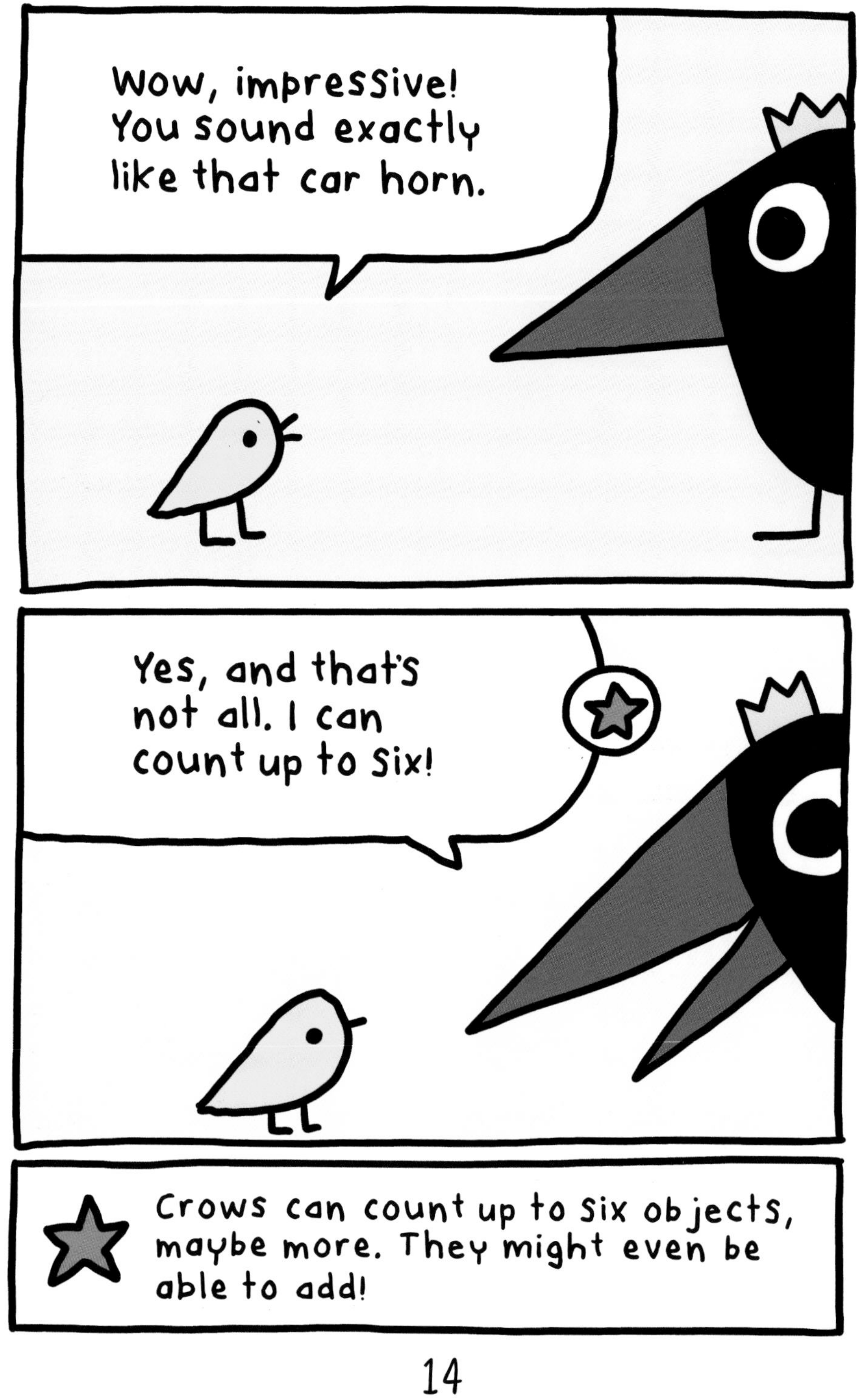
Wow, impressive! You sound exactly like that car horn.
Yes, and that's not all. I can count up to six!

Crows can count up to six objects, maybe more. They might even be able to add!

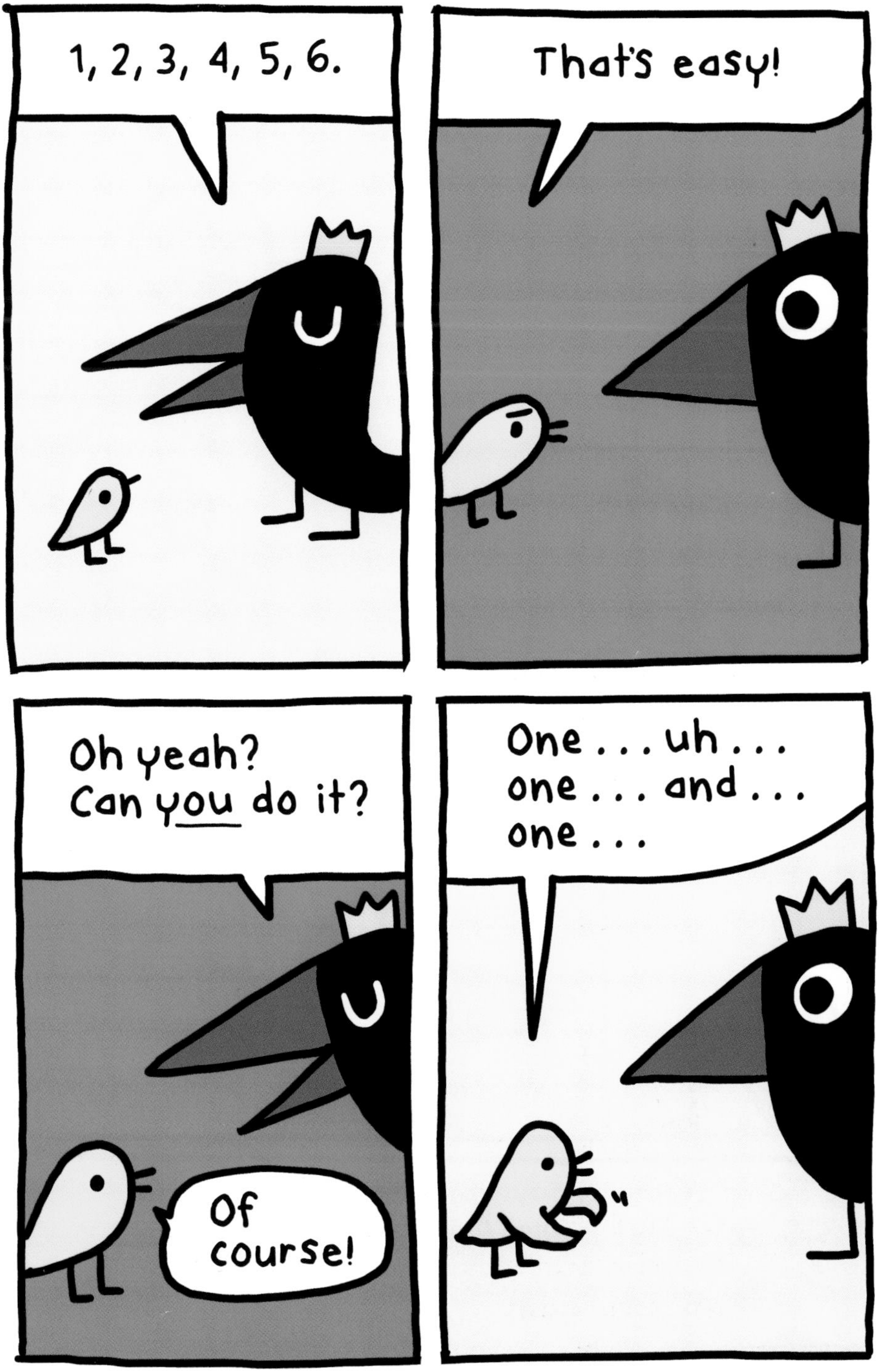
1, 2, 3, 4, 5, 6.
That's easy!
Oh yeah?
Can you do it?
Of course!
One . . . uh . . .
one . . . and . . .
one . . .

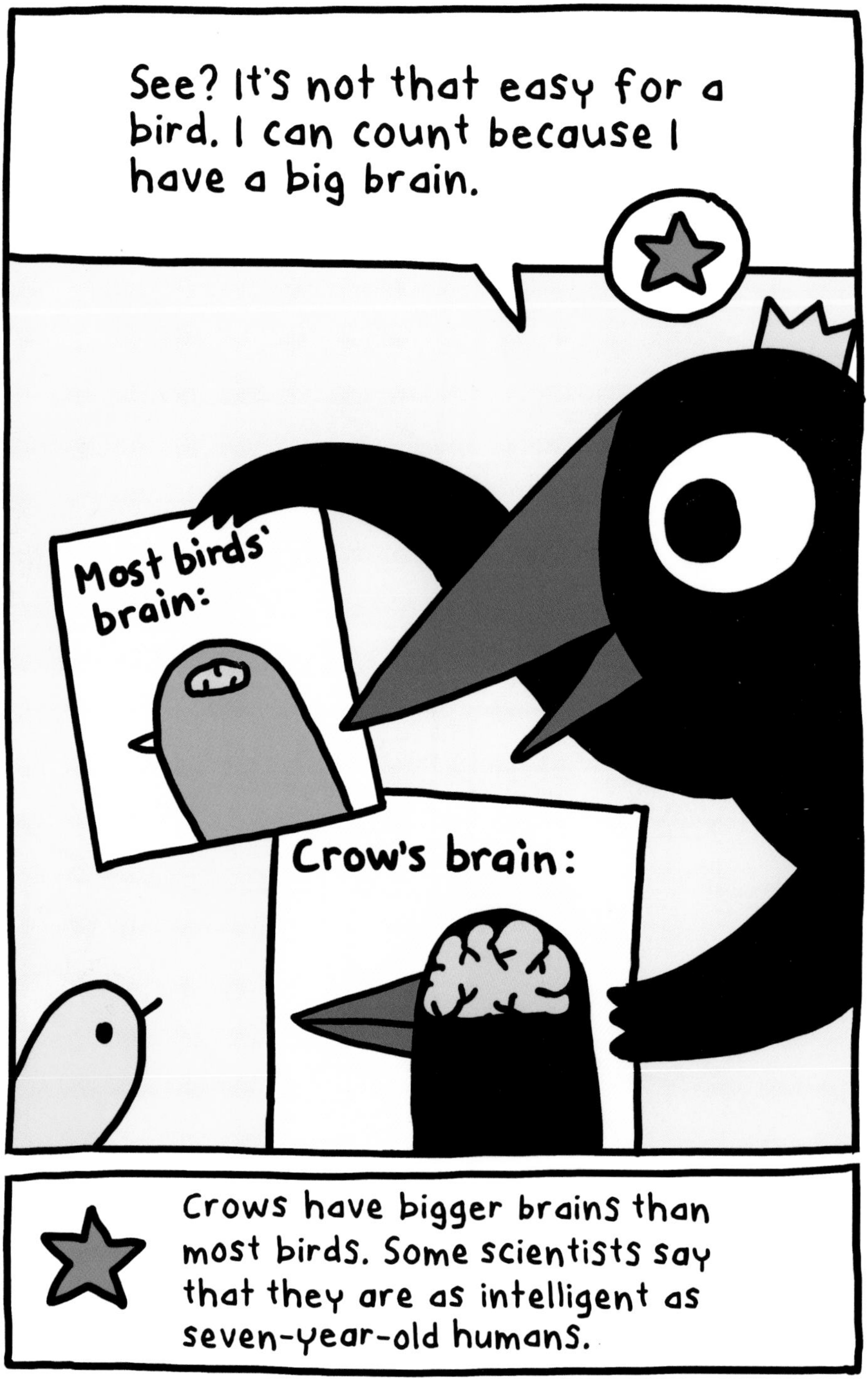
See? It's not that easy for a bird. I can count because I have a big brain.
Most birds' brain:
Crow's brain:
Crows have bigger brains than most birds. Some scientists say that they are as intelligent as seven-year-old humans.

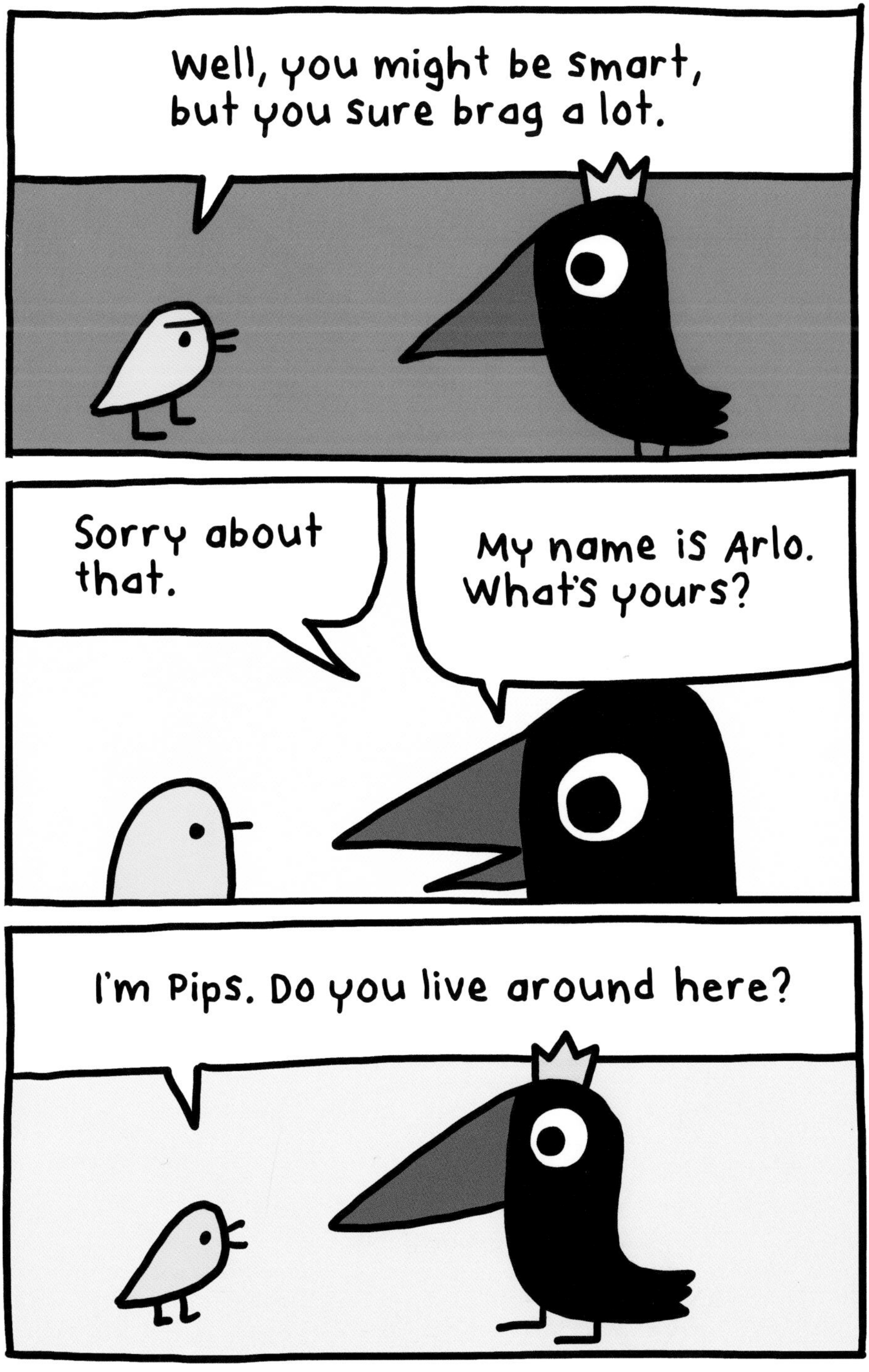
Well, you might be smart, but you sure brag a lot.
Sorry about that.
My name is Arlo. What's yours?
I'm Pips. Do you live around here?

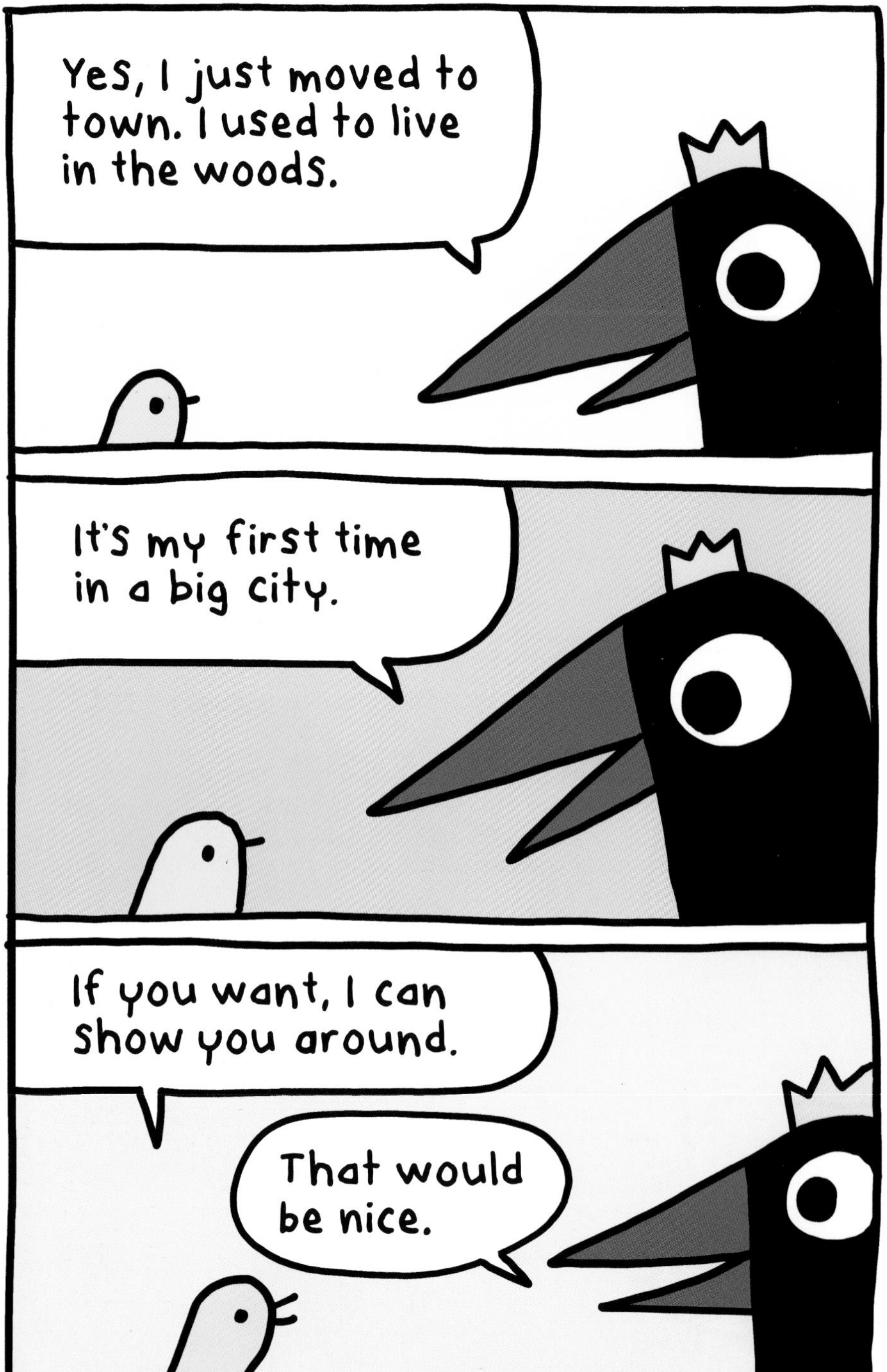
Yes, I just moved to town. I used to live in the woods.
It's my first time in a big city.
If you want, I can show you around.
That would be nice.

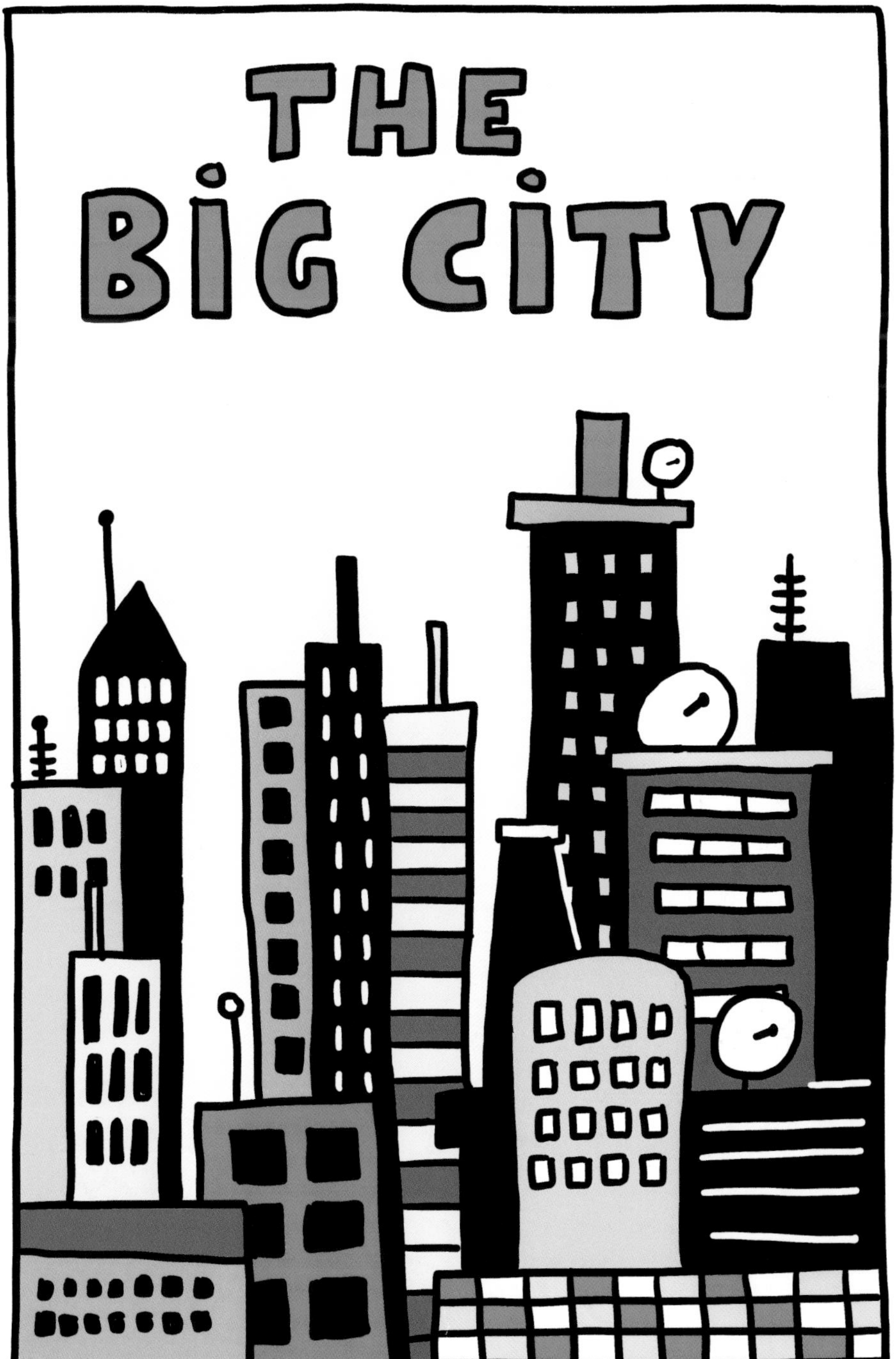
THE
BIG CITY

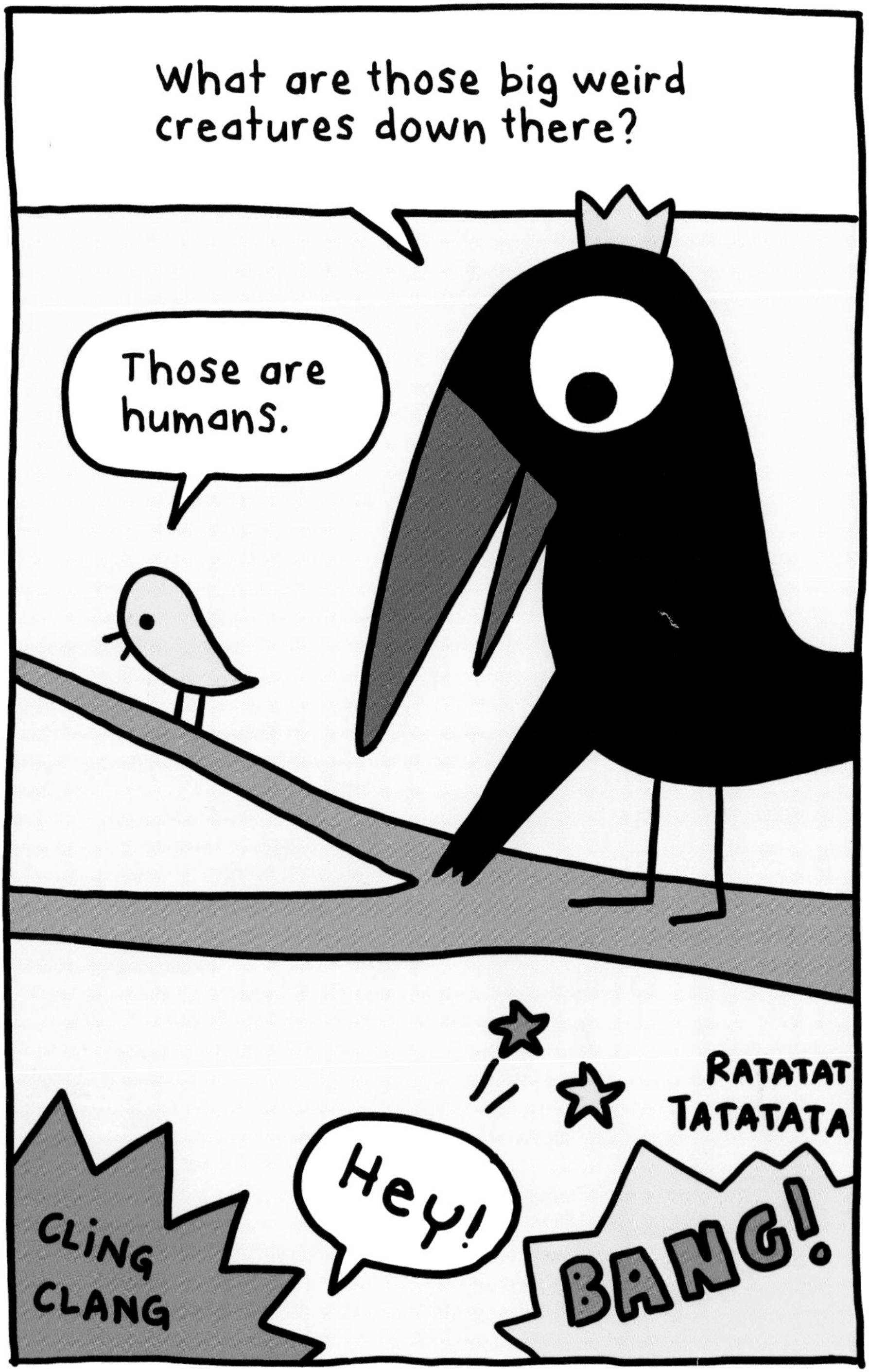
What are those big weird creatures down there?
Those are humans.
RATATAT TATATATA
Hey!
CLING CLANG
BANG!

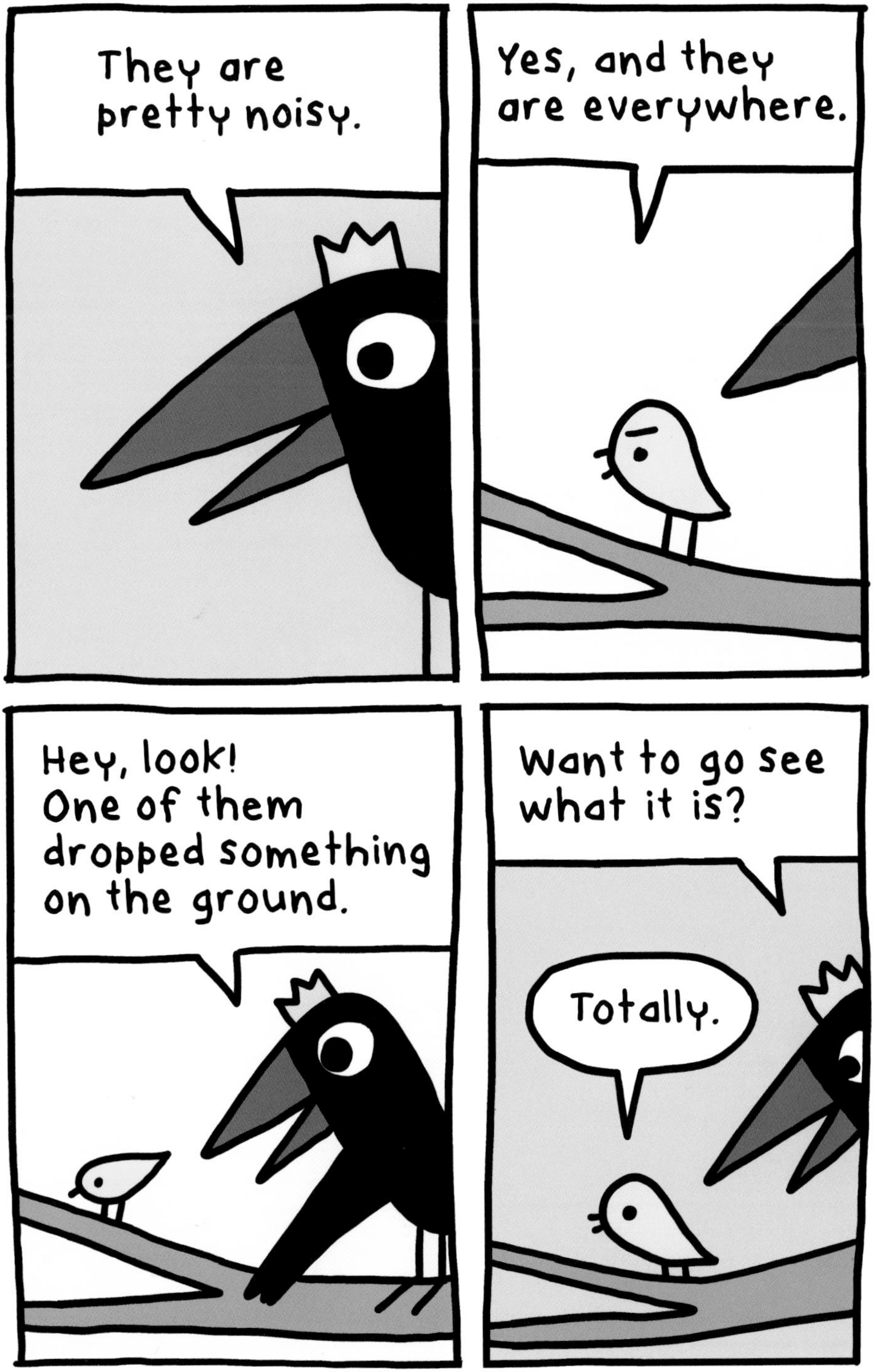
They are pretty noisy.
Yes, and they are everywhere.
Hey, look! One of them dropped something on the ground.
Want to go see what it is?
Totally.

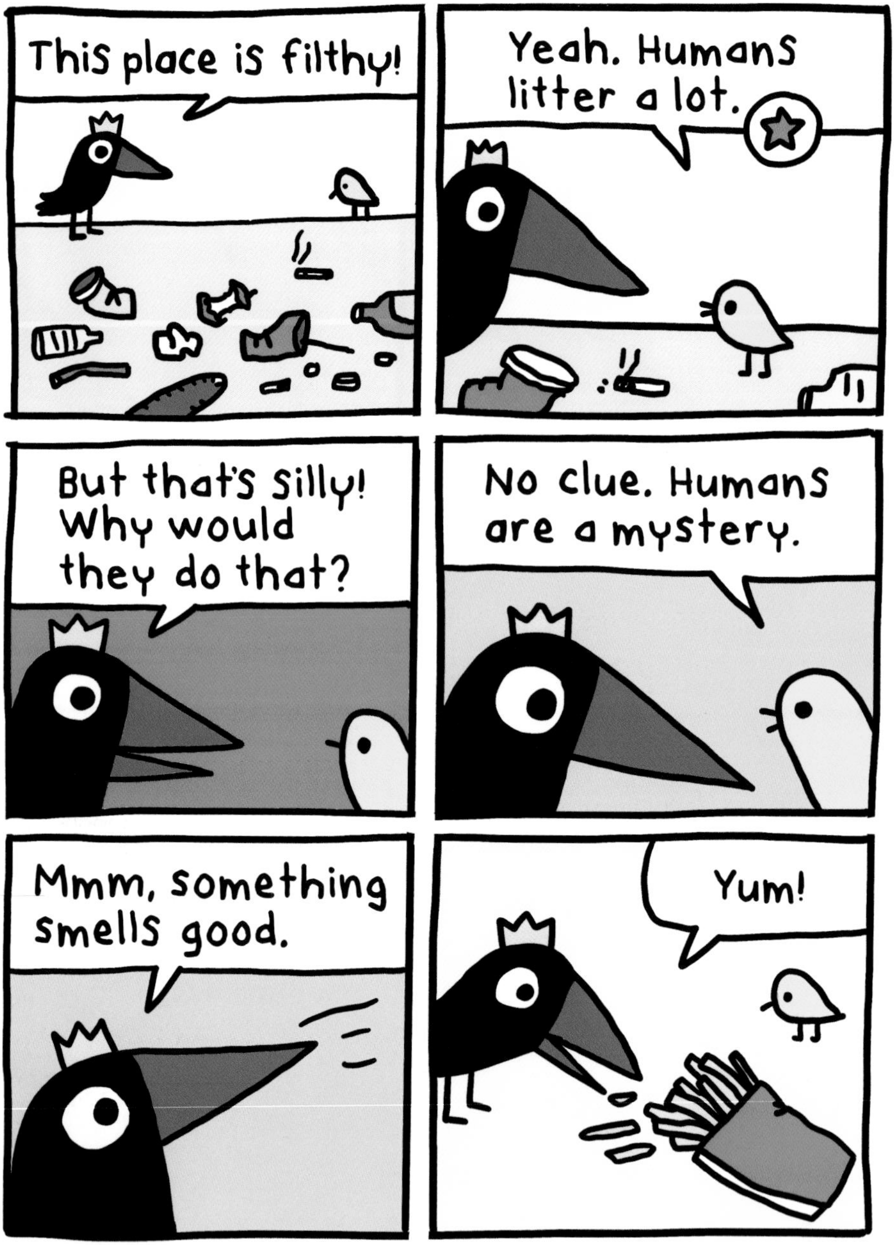
This place is filthy!
Yeah. Humans litter a lot.
But that's silly! Why would they do that?
No clue. Humans are a mystery.
Mmm, something smells good.
Yum!

★ Humans do litter a lot. (Sigh.)

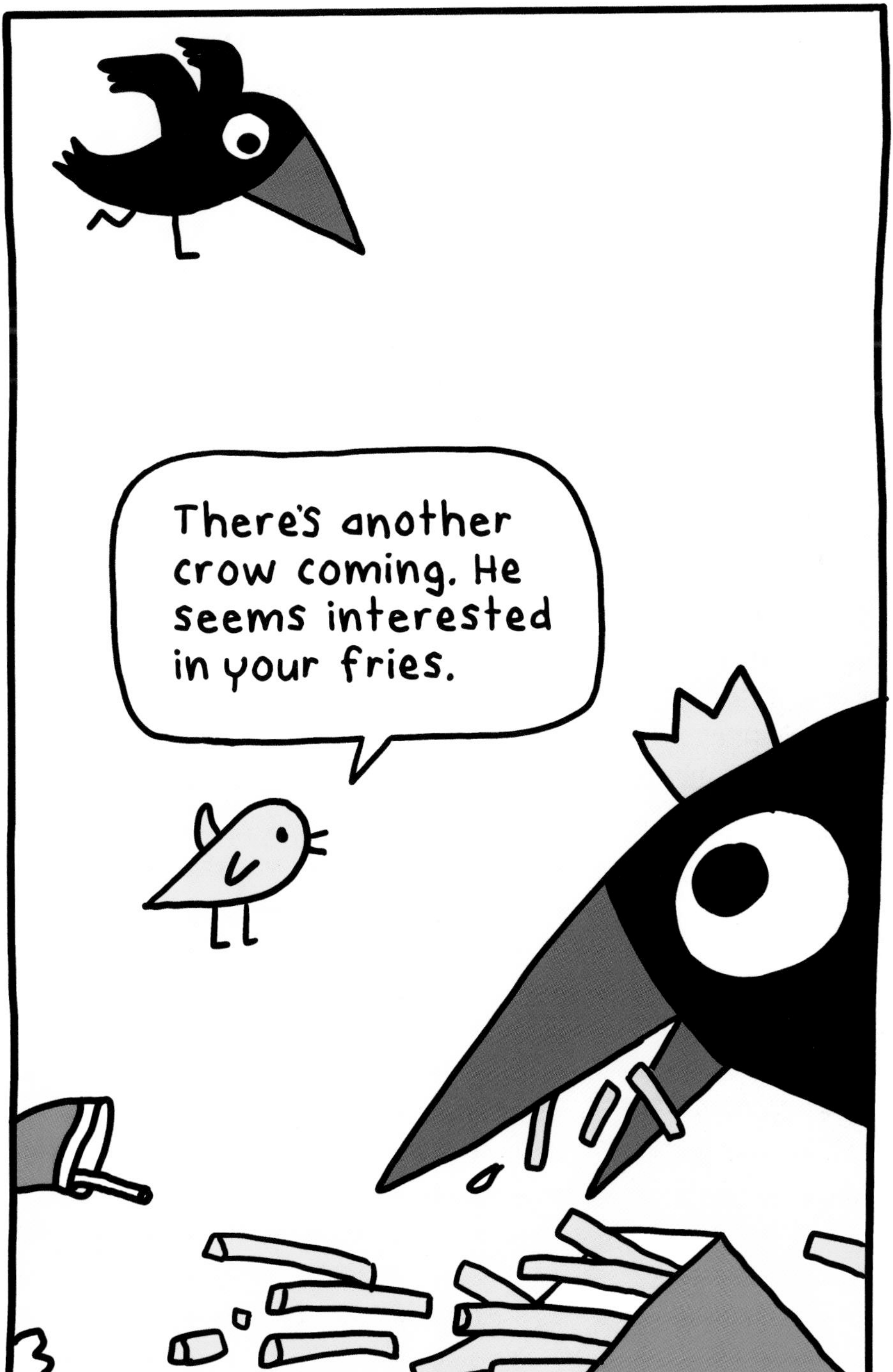
There's another crow coming. He seems interested in your fries.

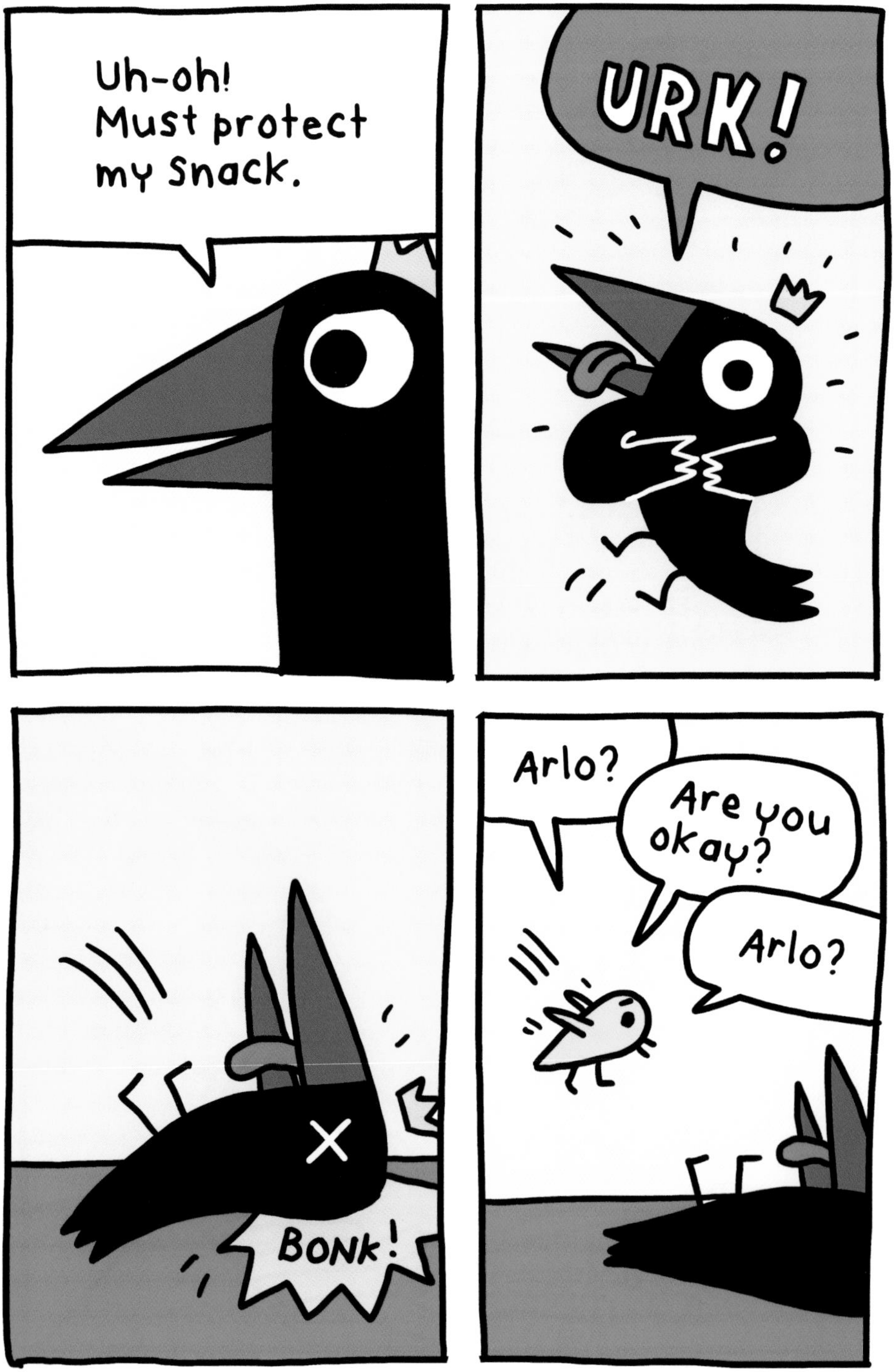
Uh-oh!
Must protect
my snack.
URK!
BONK!
Arlo?
Are you
okay?
Arlo?

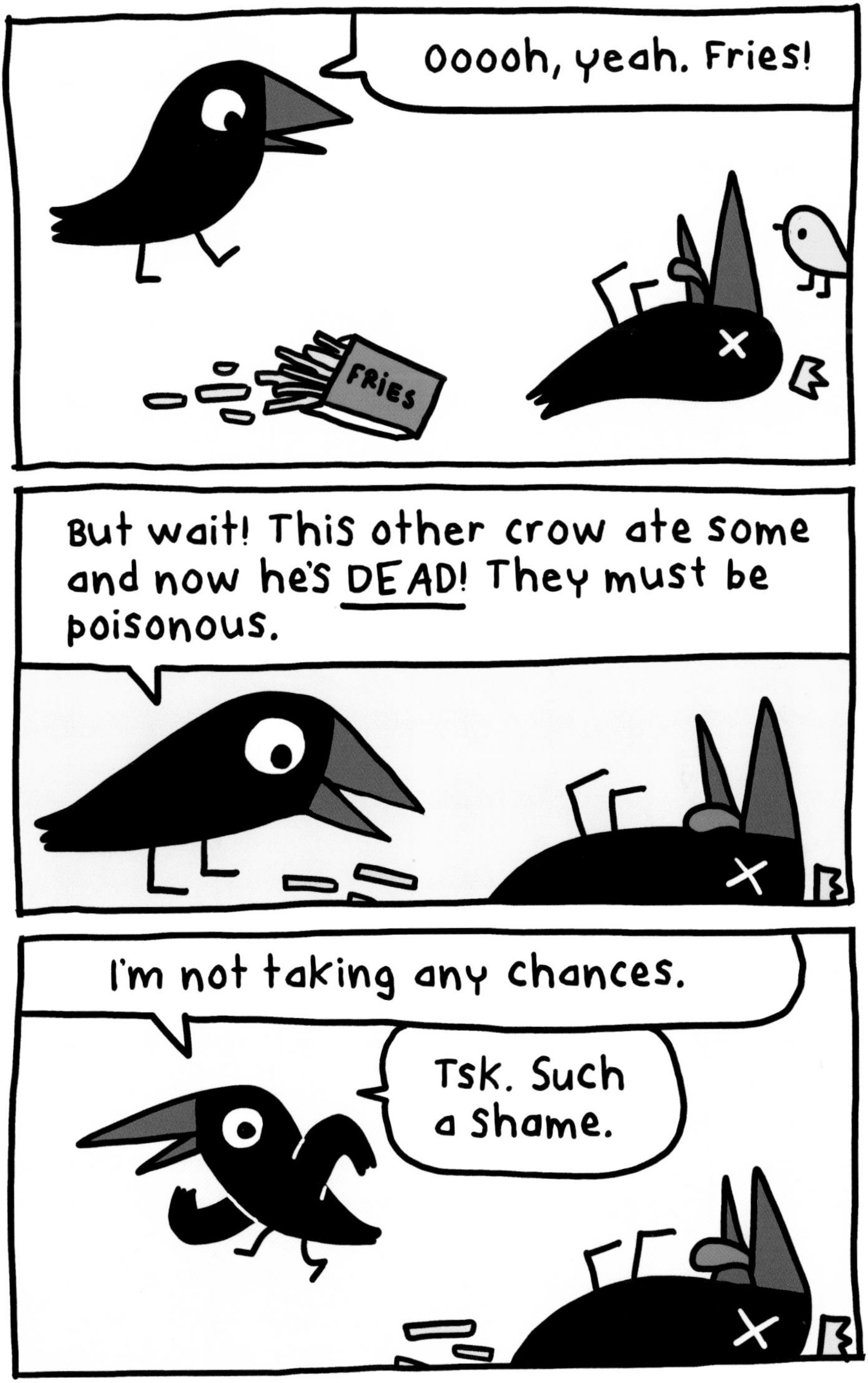
Ooooh, yeah. Fries!
FRIES
But wait! This other crow ate some and now he's DEAD! They must be poisonous.
I'm not taking any chances.
Tsk. Such a shame.

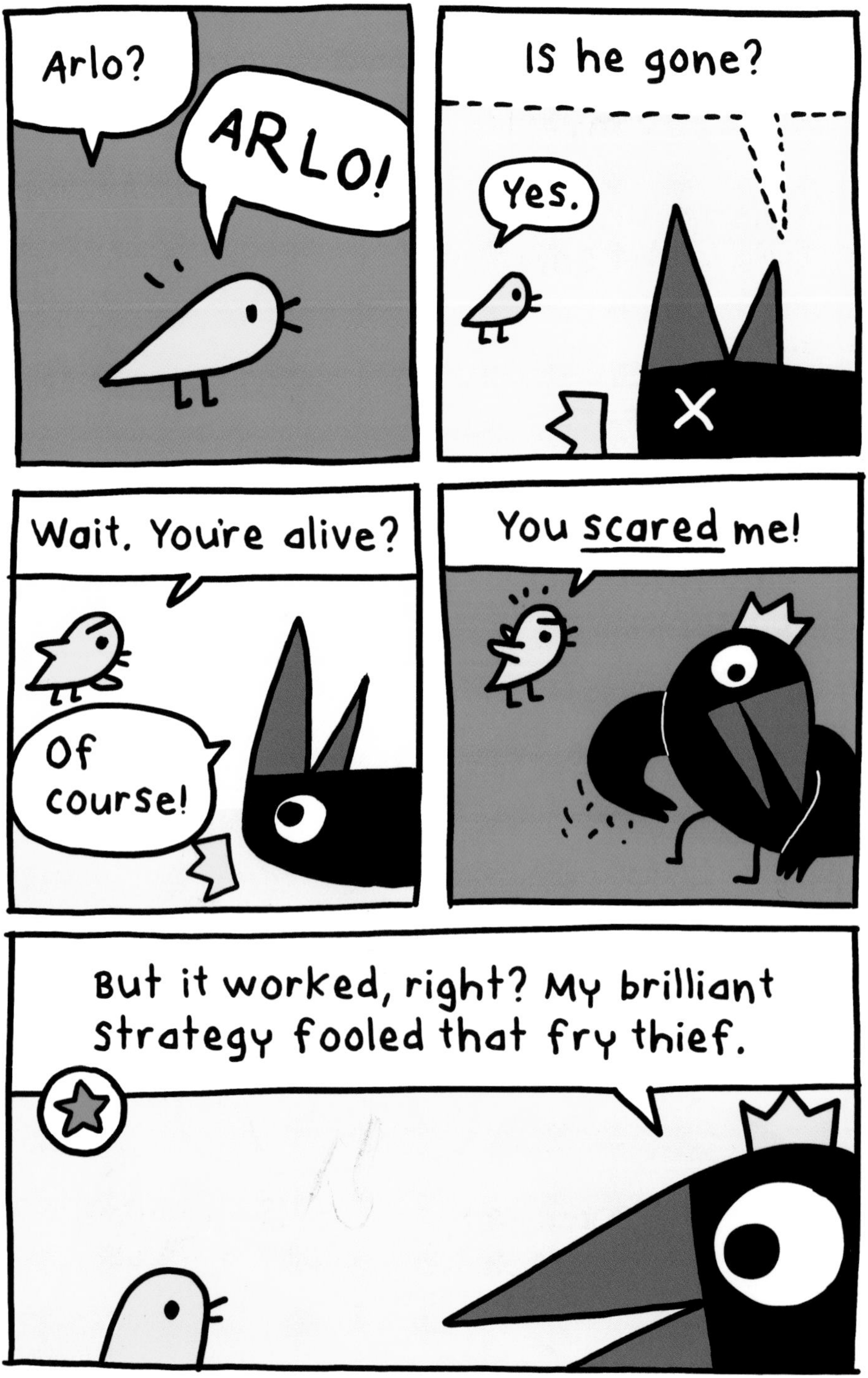
Arlo?
ARLO!
Is he gone?
Yes.
Wait. You're alive?
Of course!
You scared me!
But it worked, right? My brilliant strategy fooled that fry thief.

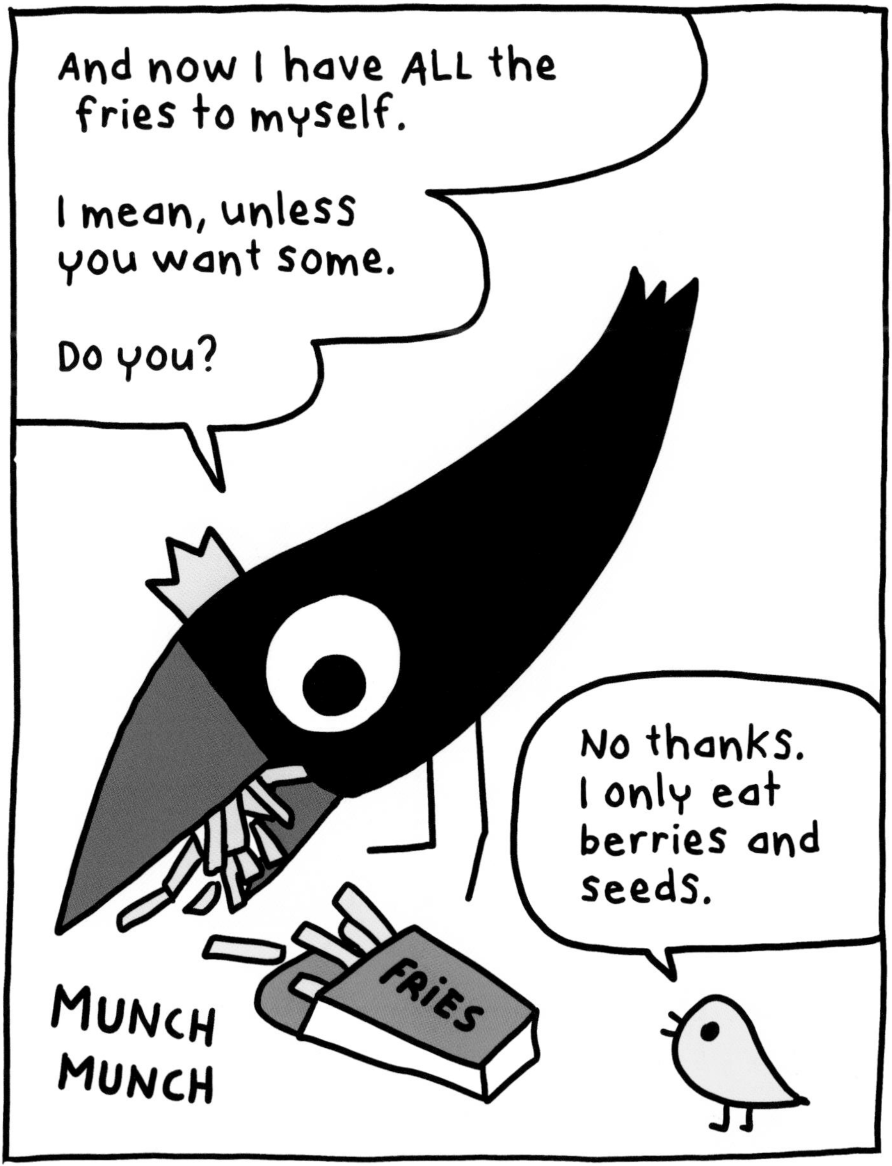
And now I have ALL the fries to myself.
I mean, unless you want some.
Do you?
MUNCH MUNCH
FRIES
No thanks. I only eat berries and seeds.

Some crows have been seen playing dead to fool other crows and keep food for themselves.

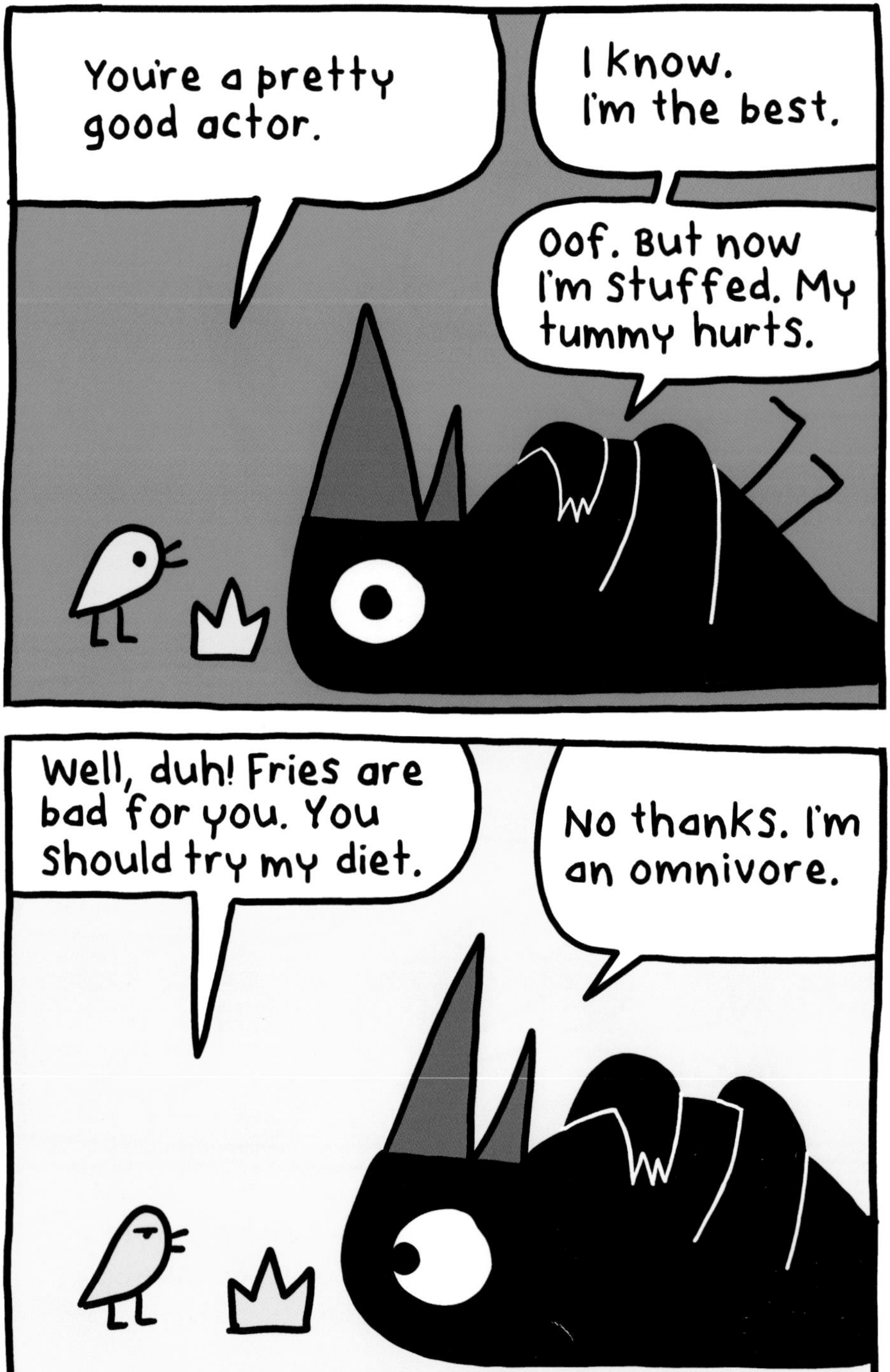
You're a pretty good actor.
I know. I'm the best.
Oof. But now I'm stuffed. My tummy hurts.
Well, duh! Fries are bad for you. You should try my diet.
No thanks. I'm an omnivore.

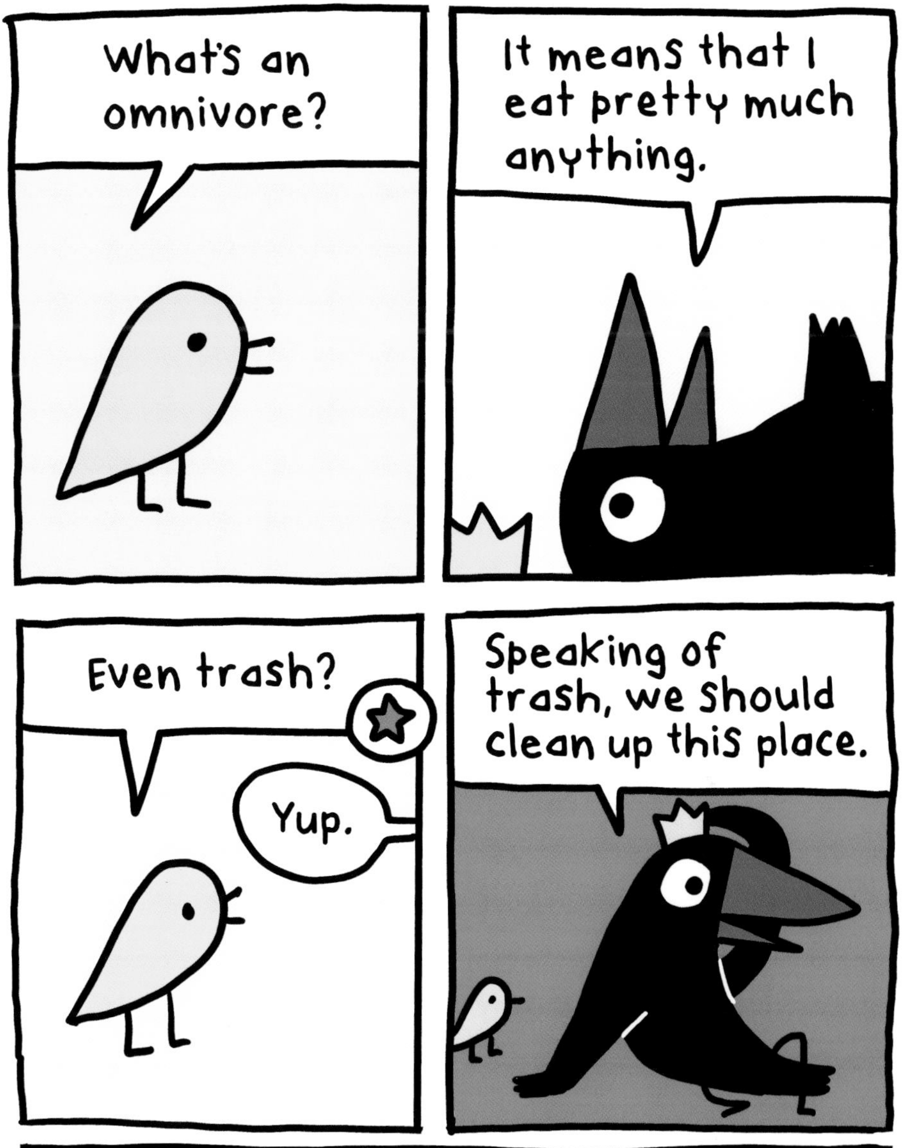
What's an omnivore?
It means that I eat pretty much anything.
Even trash?
Yup.
Speaking of trash, we should clean up this place.

Crows eat many things: seeds, fruit, small mammals, frogs, bugs, lizards, worms, eggs, nuts, mollusks, human food scraps . . . and yes, trash.

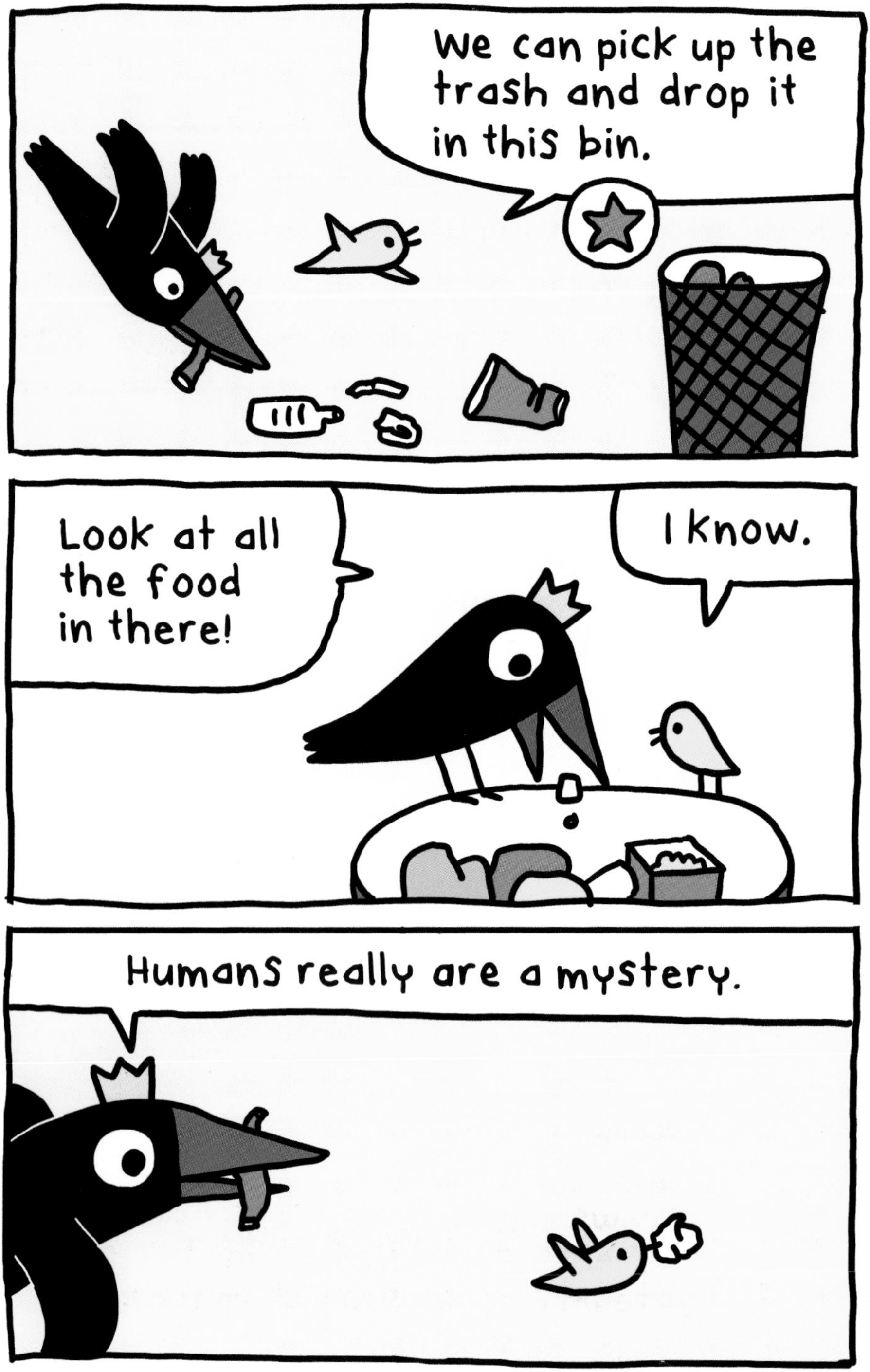
We can pick up the trash and drop it in this bin.
Look at all the food in there!
I know.
Humans really are a mystery.

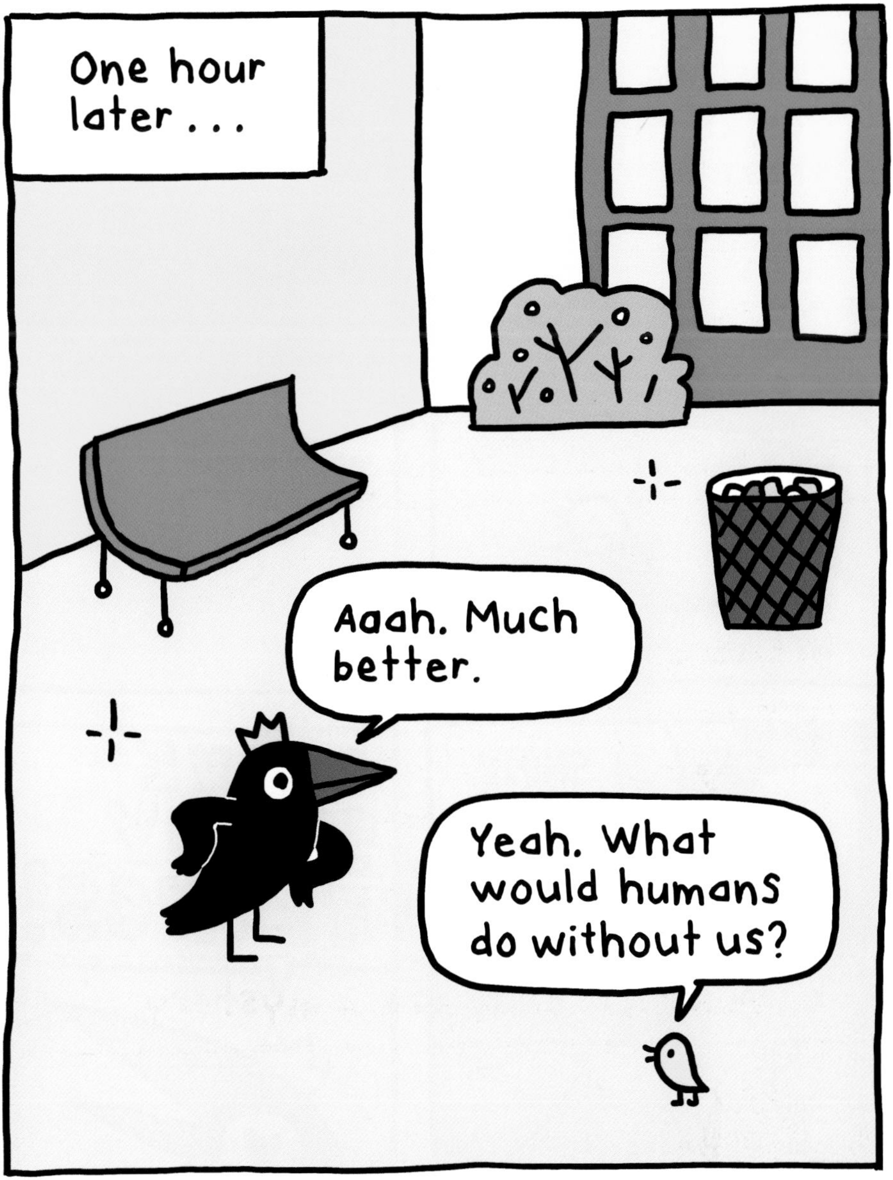
One hour later . . .
Aaah. Much better.
Yeah. What would humans do without us?

Crows can be taught tricks!
A French theme park trained
a team of crows to pick up trash.

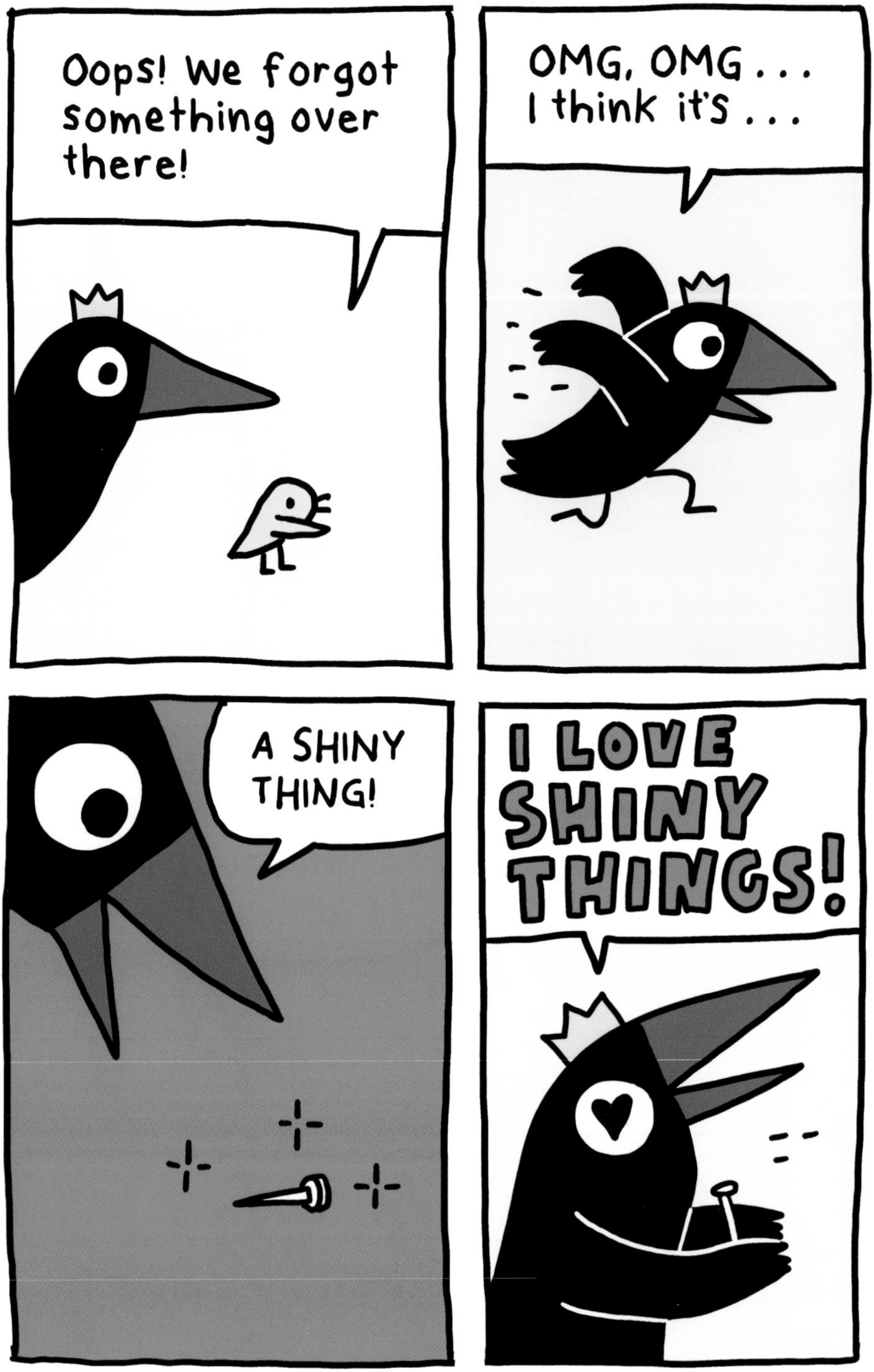
Oops! We forgot something over there!
OMG, OMG . . . I think it's . . .
A SHINY THING!
I LOVE SHINY THINGS!

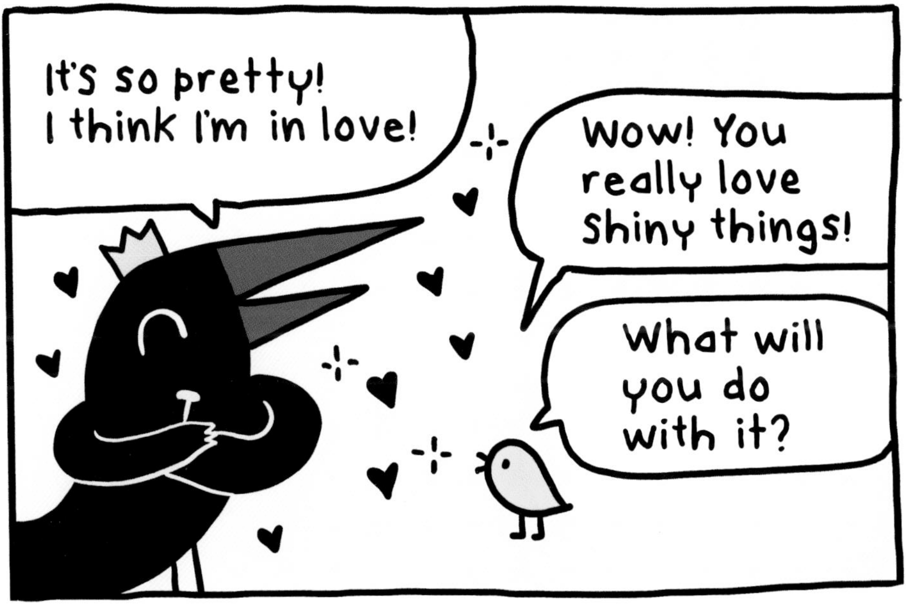
It's so pretty!
I think I'm in love!
Wow! You really love shiny things!
What will you do with it?

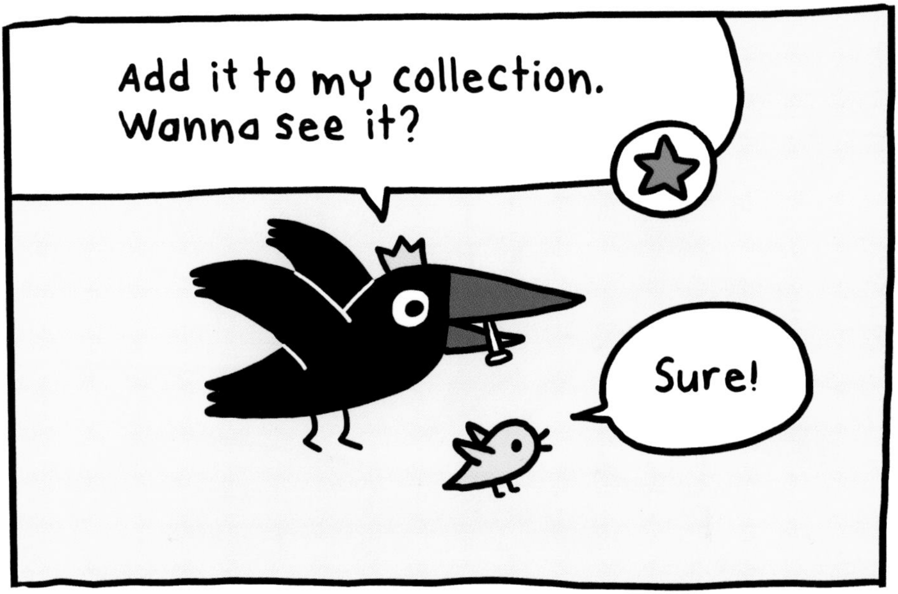
Add it to my collection. Wanna see it?
Sure!

★ Crows have a reputation for liking and collecting shiny objects.

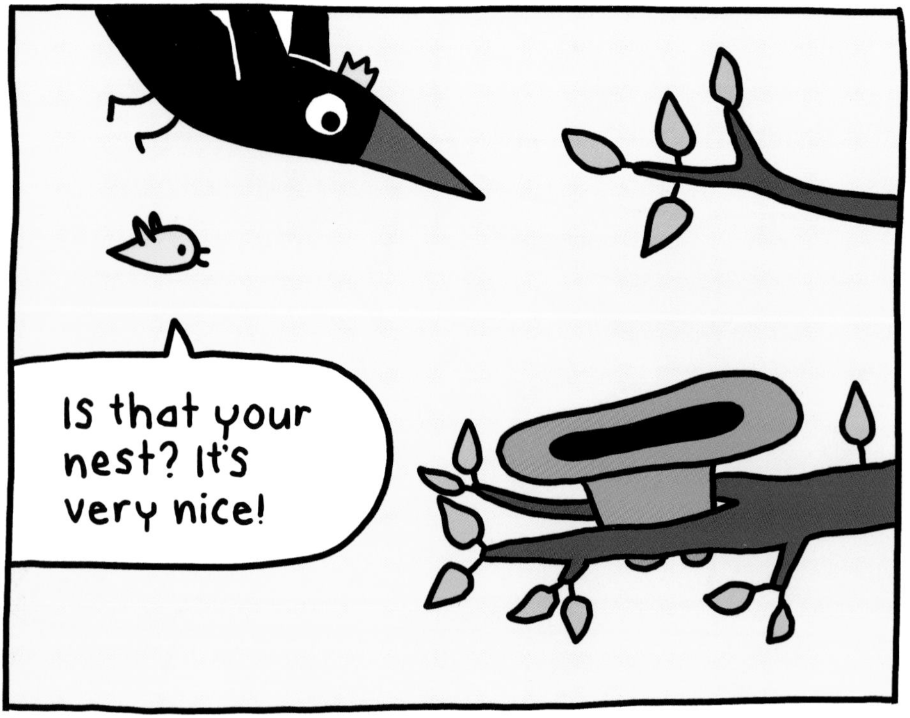
Is that your nest? It's very nice!

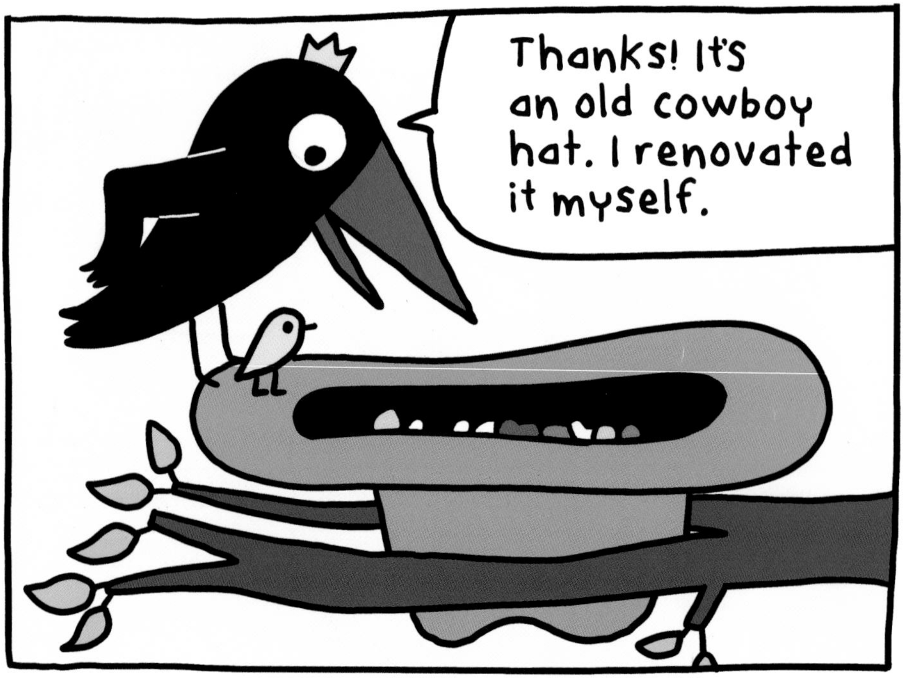
Thanks! It's an old cowboy hat. I renovated it myself.

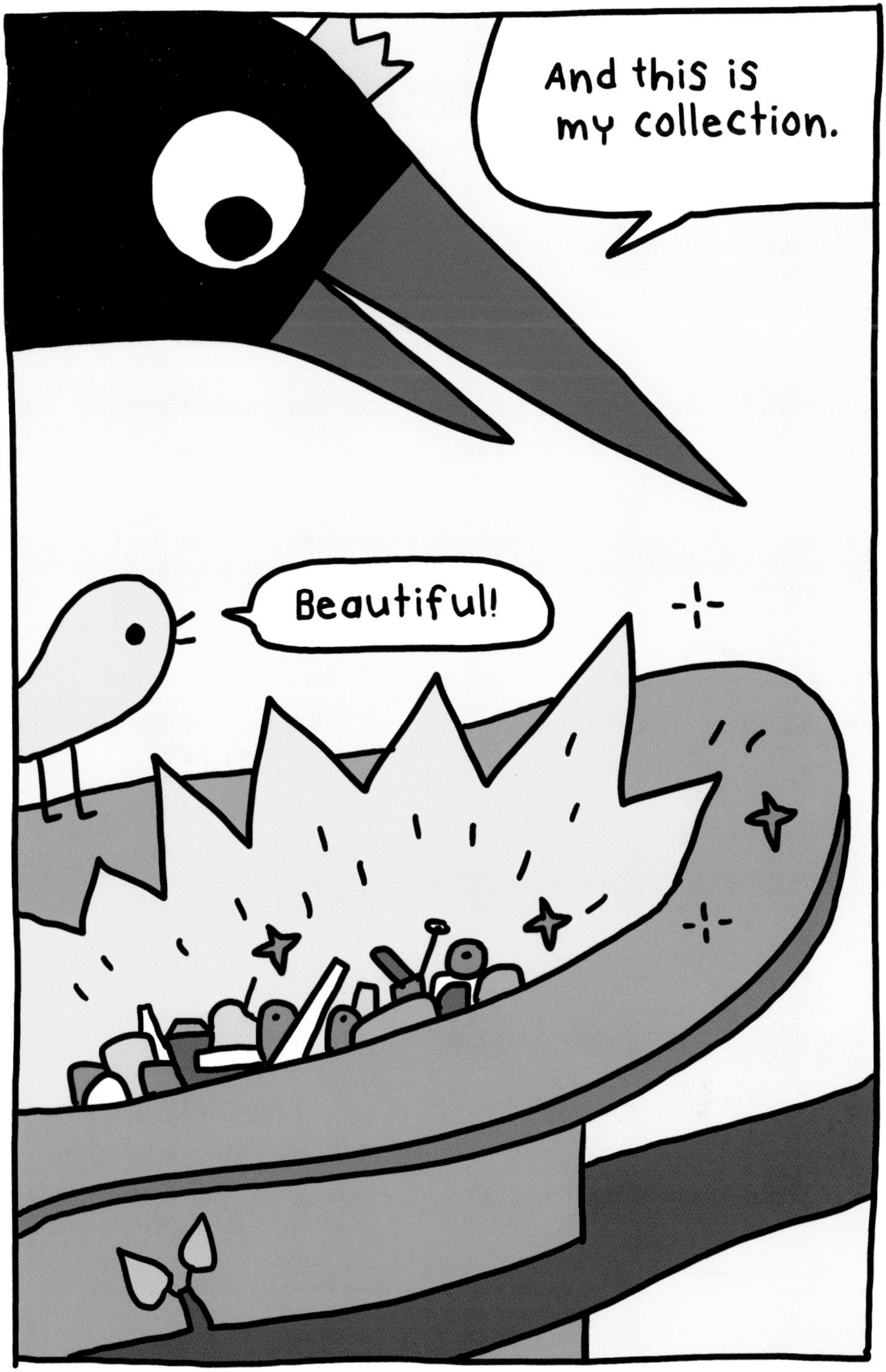
And this is my collection.
Beautiful!

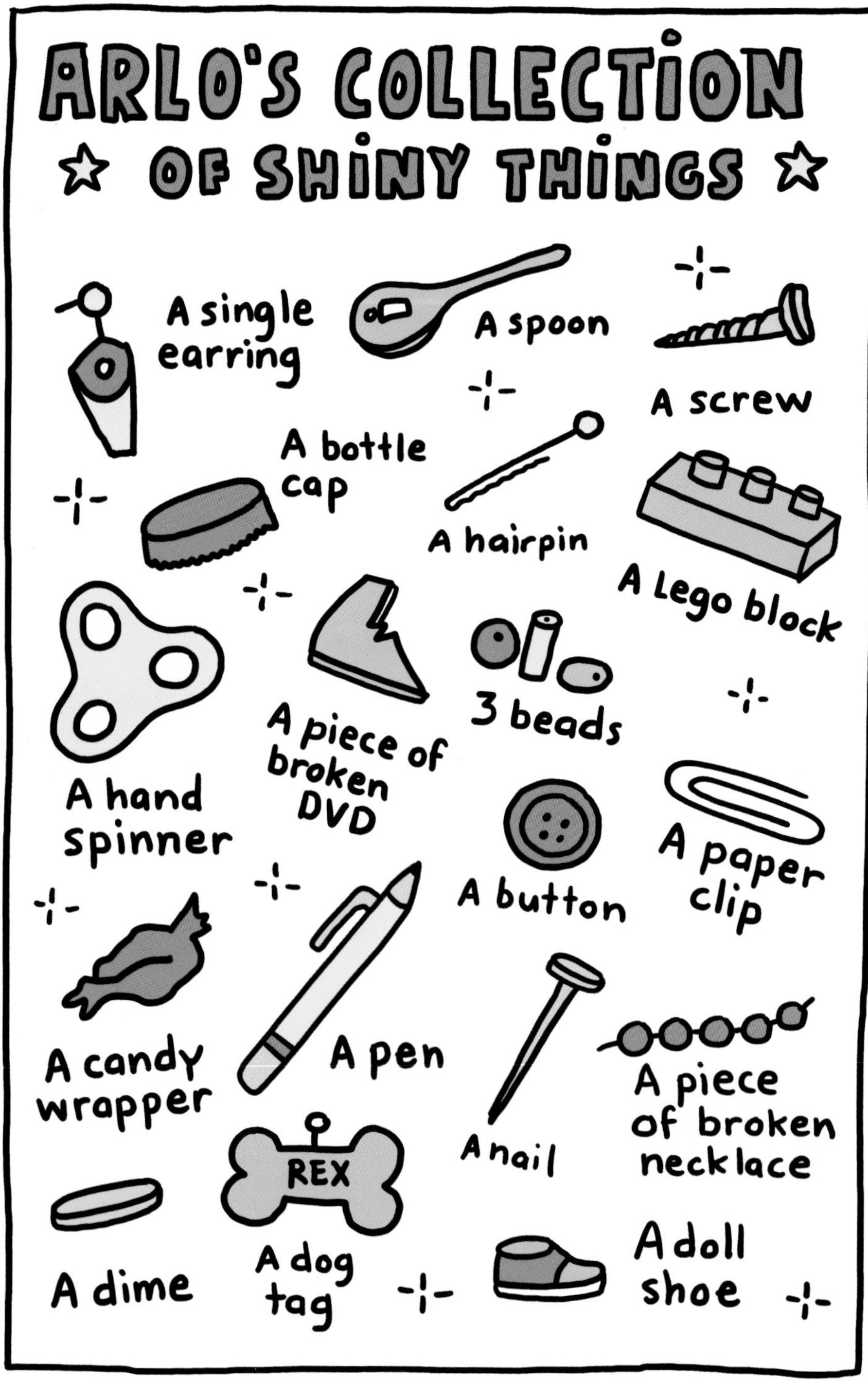
ARLO'S COLLECTION
OF SHINY THINGS
A single earring
A spoon
A screw
A bottle cap
A hairpin
A Lego block
A hand spinner
A piece of broken DVD
3 beads
A button
A paper clip
A candy wrapper
A pen
A nail
A piece of broken necklace
A dime
REX
A dog tag
A doll shoe

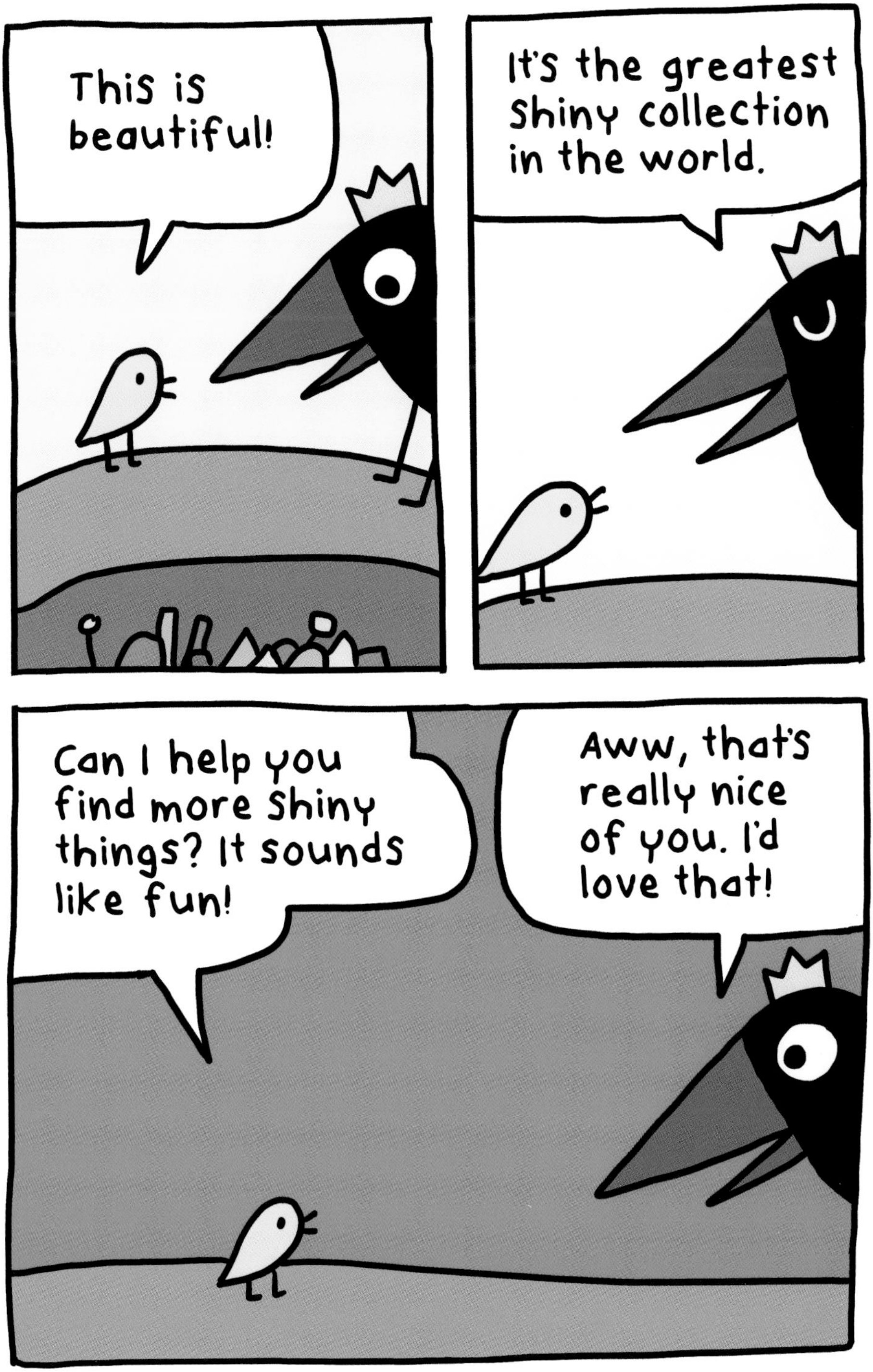
This is beautiful!
It's the greatest shiny collection in the world.
Can I help you find more shiny things? It sounds like fun!
Aww, that's really nice of you. I'd love that!

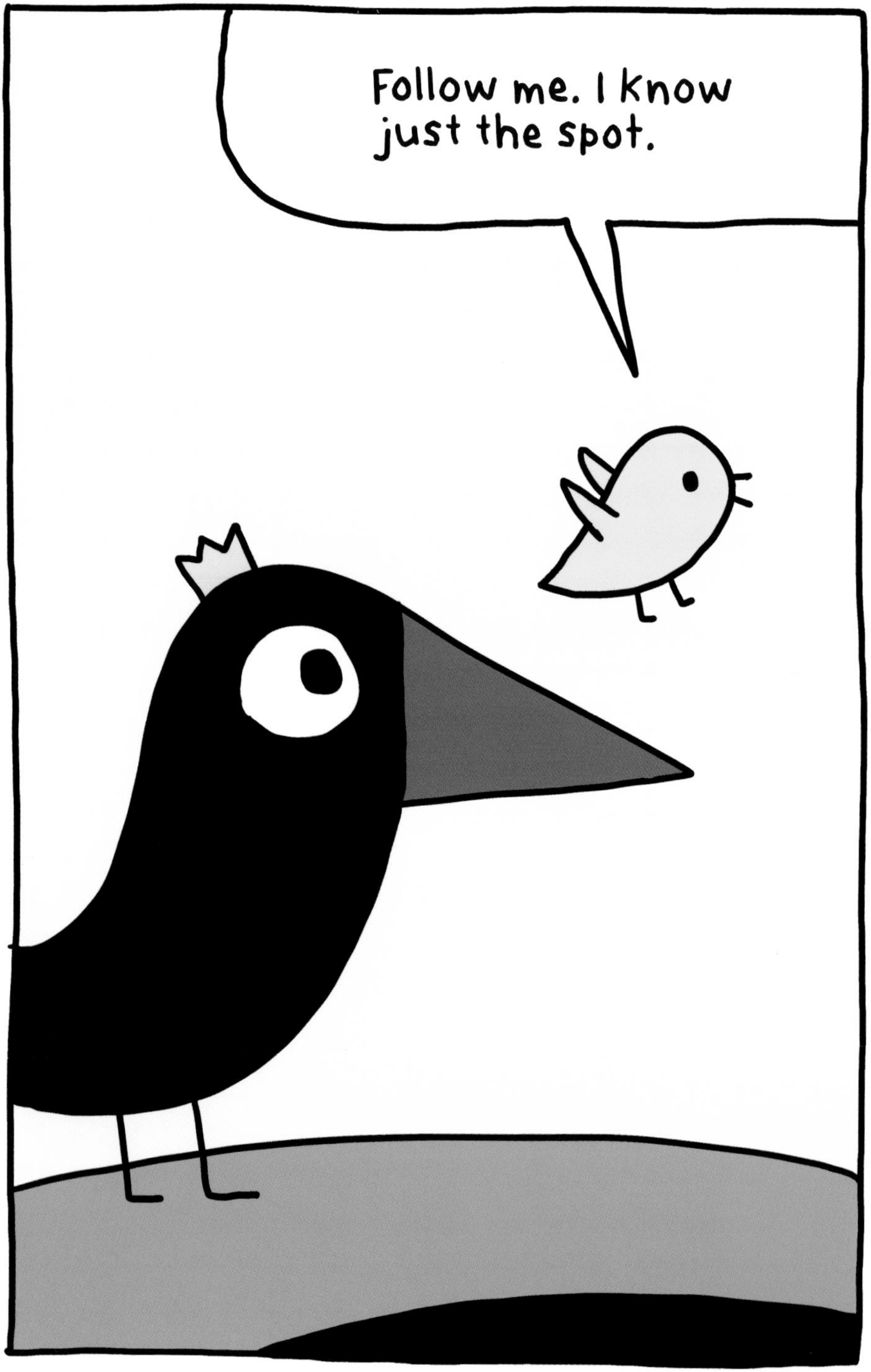
Follow me. I know just the spot.

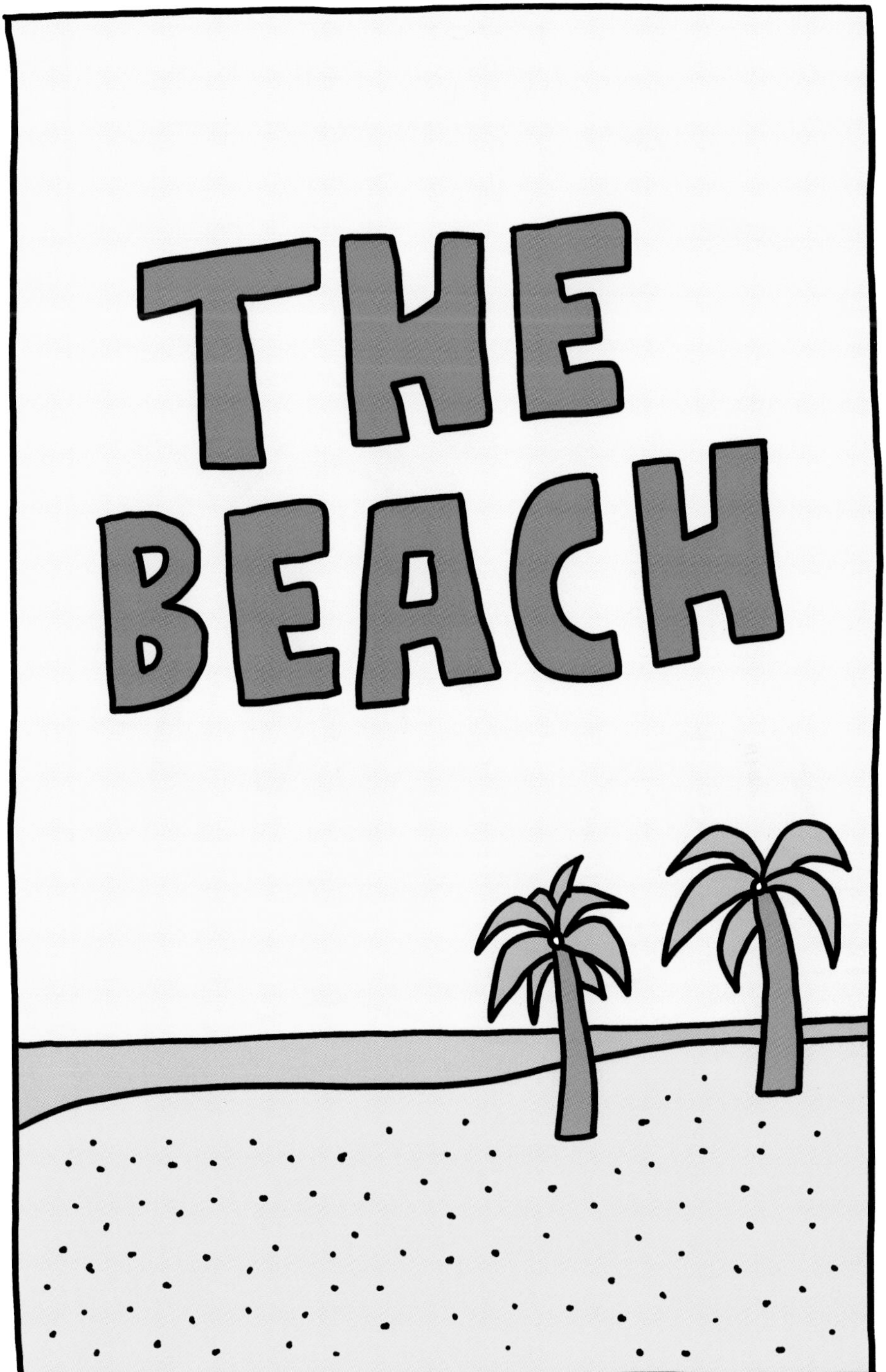
THE BEACH

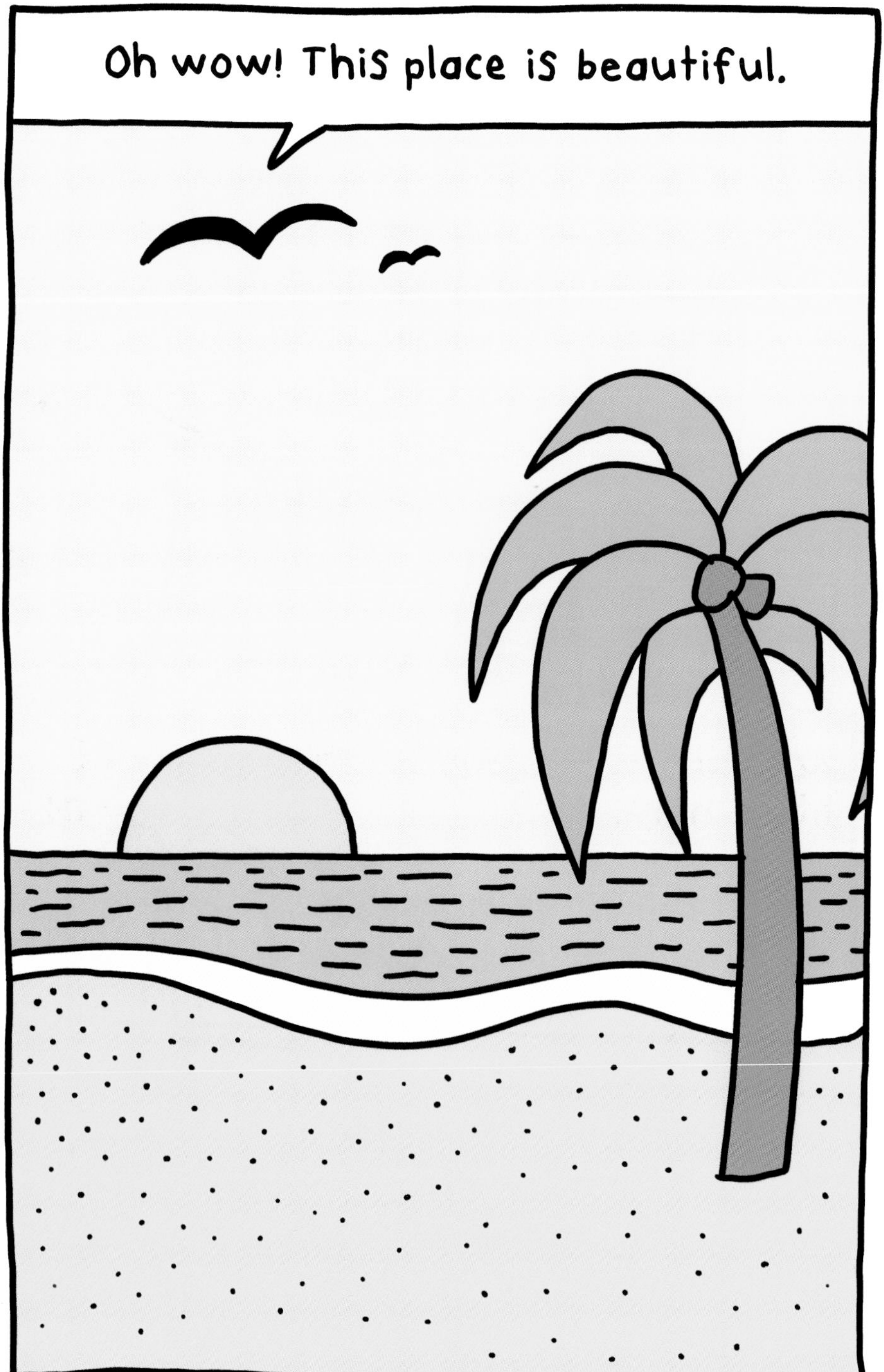
Oh wow! This place is beautiful.

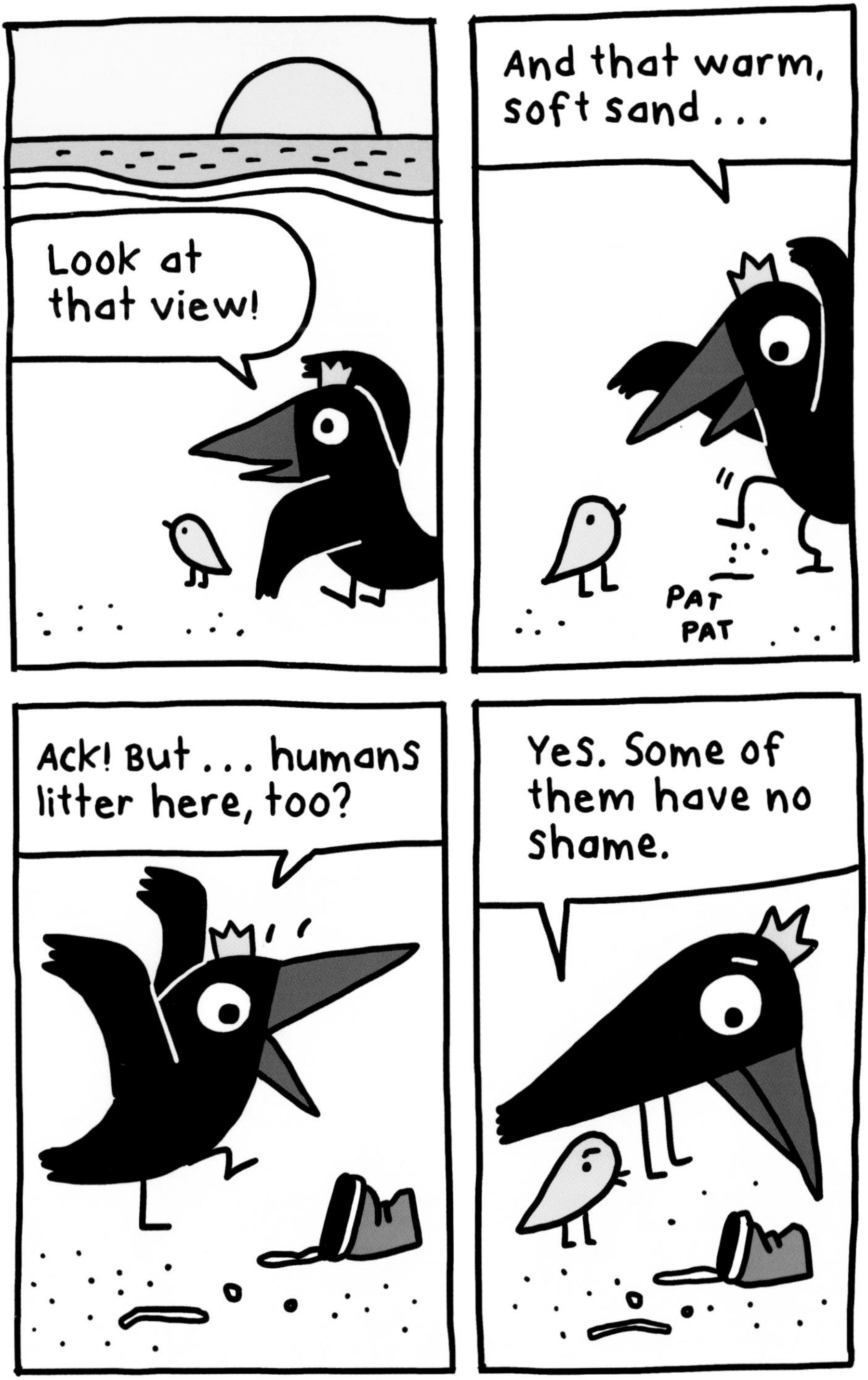
Look at that view!
And that warm, soft sand . . .
PAT PAT
ACK! But . . . humans litter here, too?
Yes. Some of them have no shame.

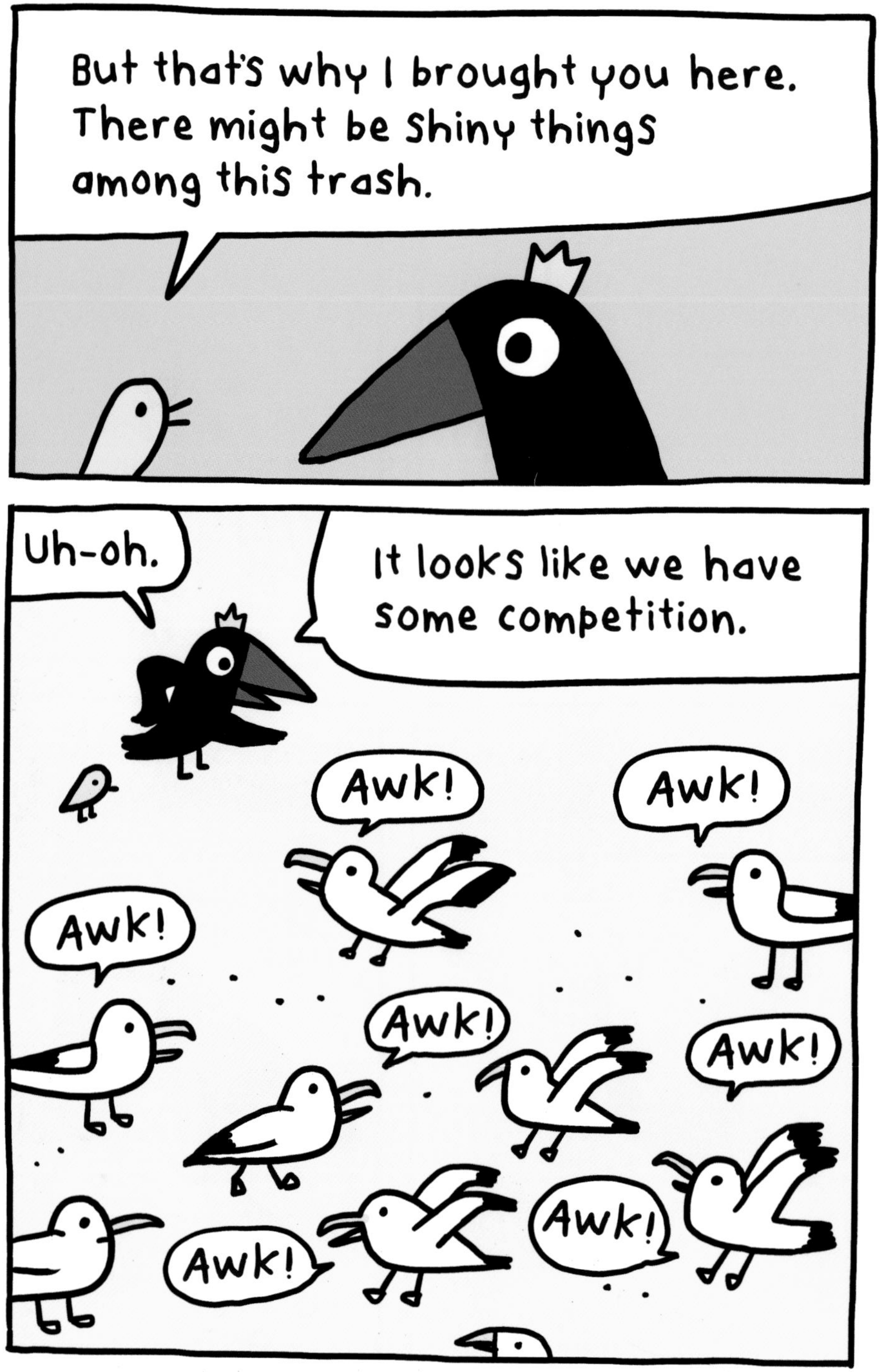
But that's why I brought you here. There might be shiny things among this trash.
Uh-oh.
It looks like we have some competition.
AWK!
AWK!
AWK!
AWK!
AWK!
AWK!
AWK!

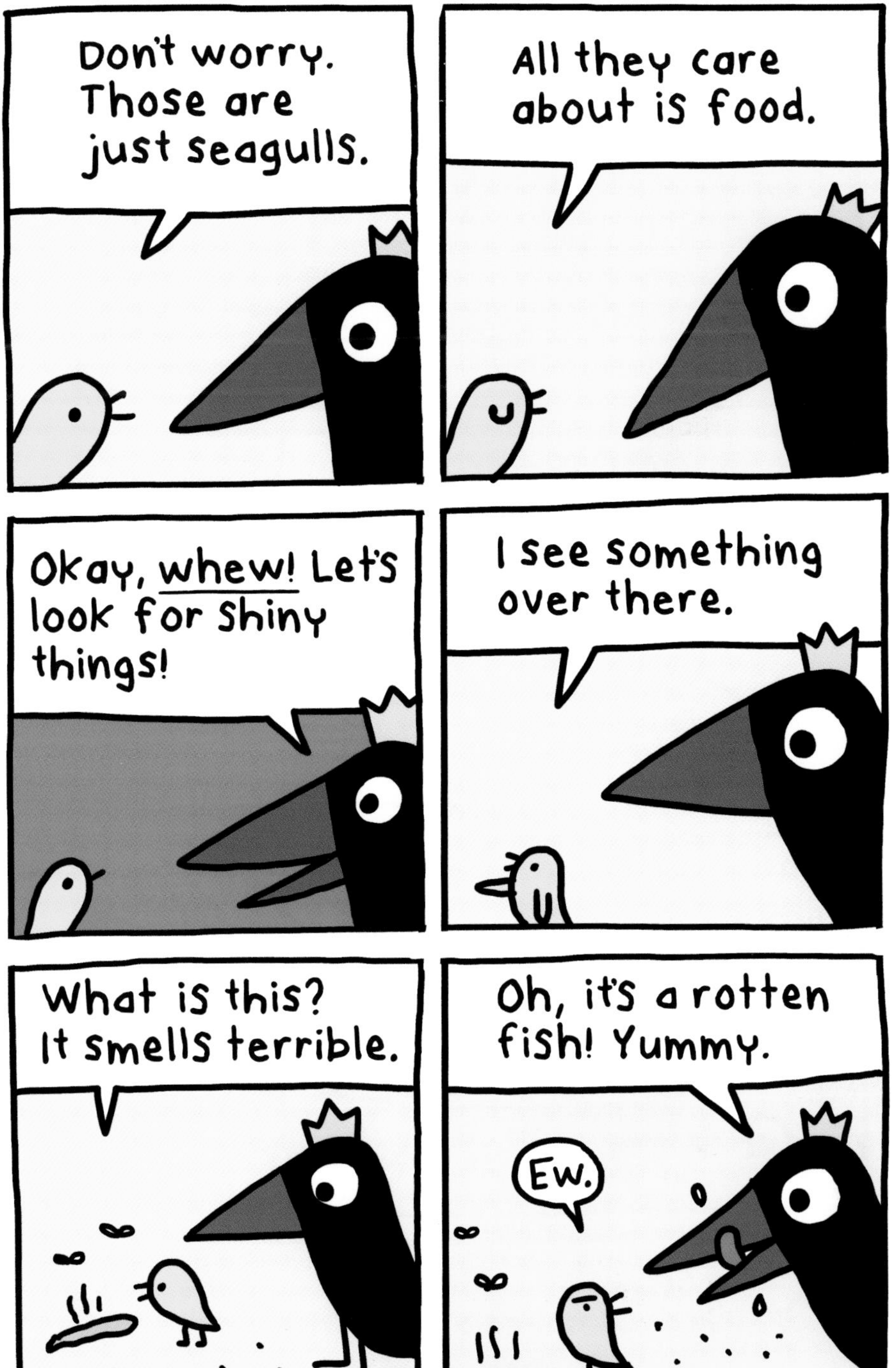
Don't worry. Those are just seagulls.
All they care about is food.
Okay, whew! Let's look for shiny things!
I see something over there.
What is this? It smells terrible.
Oh, it's a rotten fish! Yummy.
Ew.

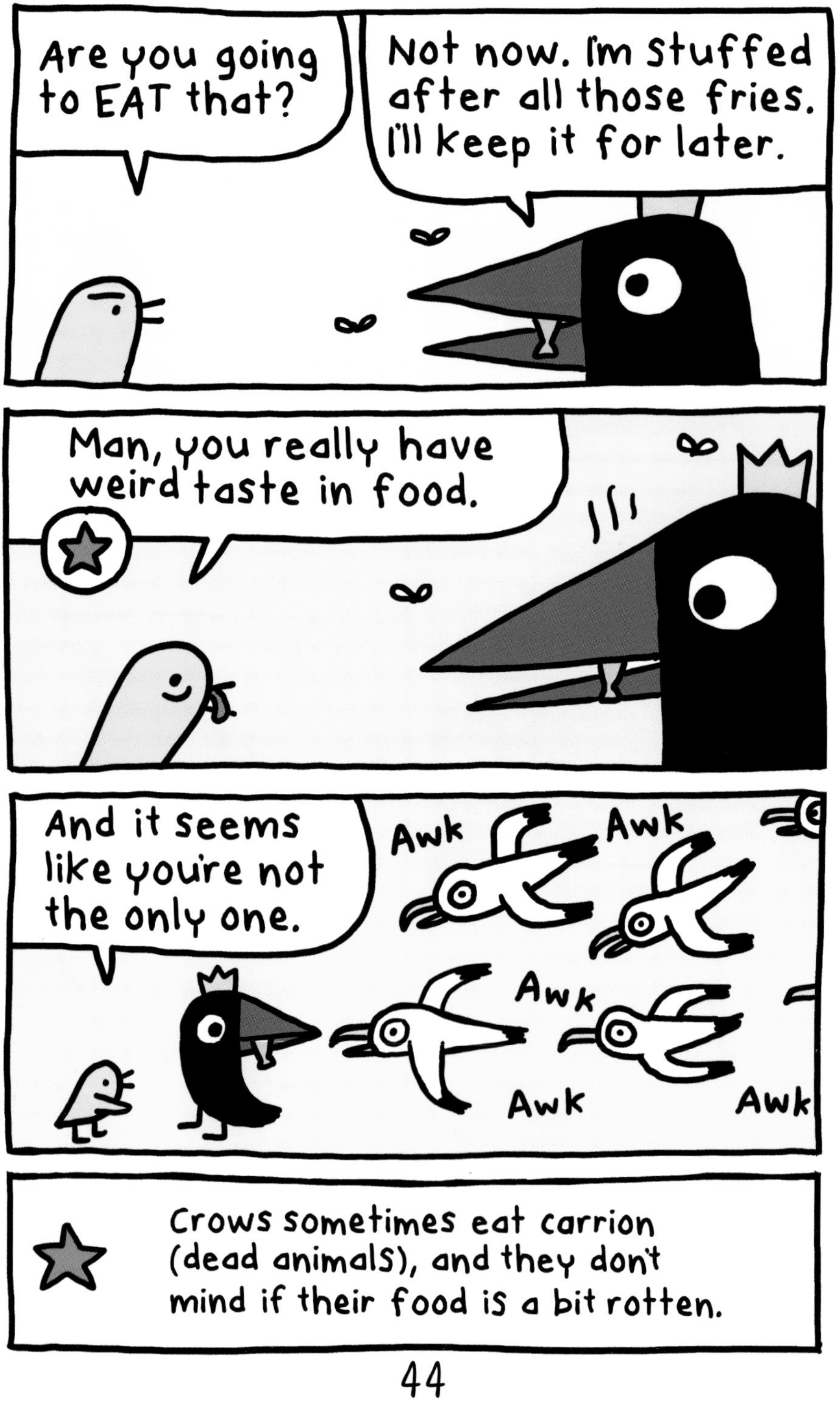

Are you going to EAT that?
Not now. I'm stuffed after all those fries. I'll keep it for later.
Man, you really have weird taste in food.
And it seems like you're not the only one.
Awk
Awk
Awk
Awk
Awk


★ Crows sometimes eat carrion (dead animals), and they don't mind if their food is a bit rotten.

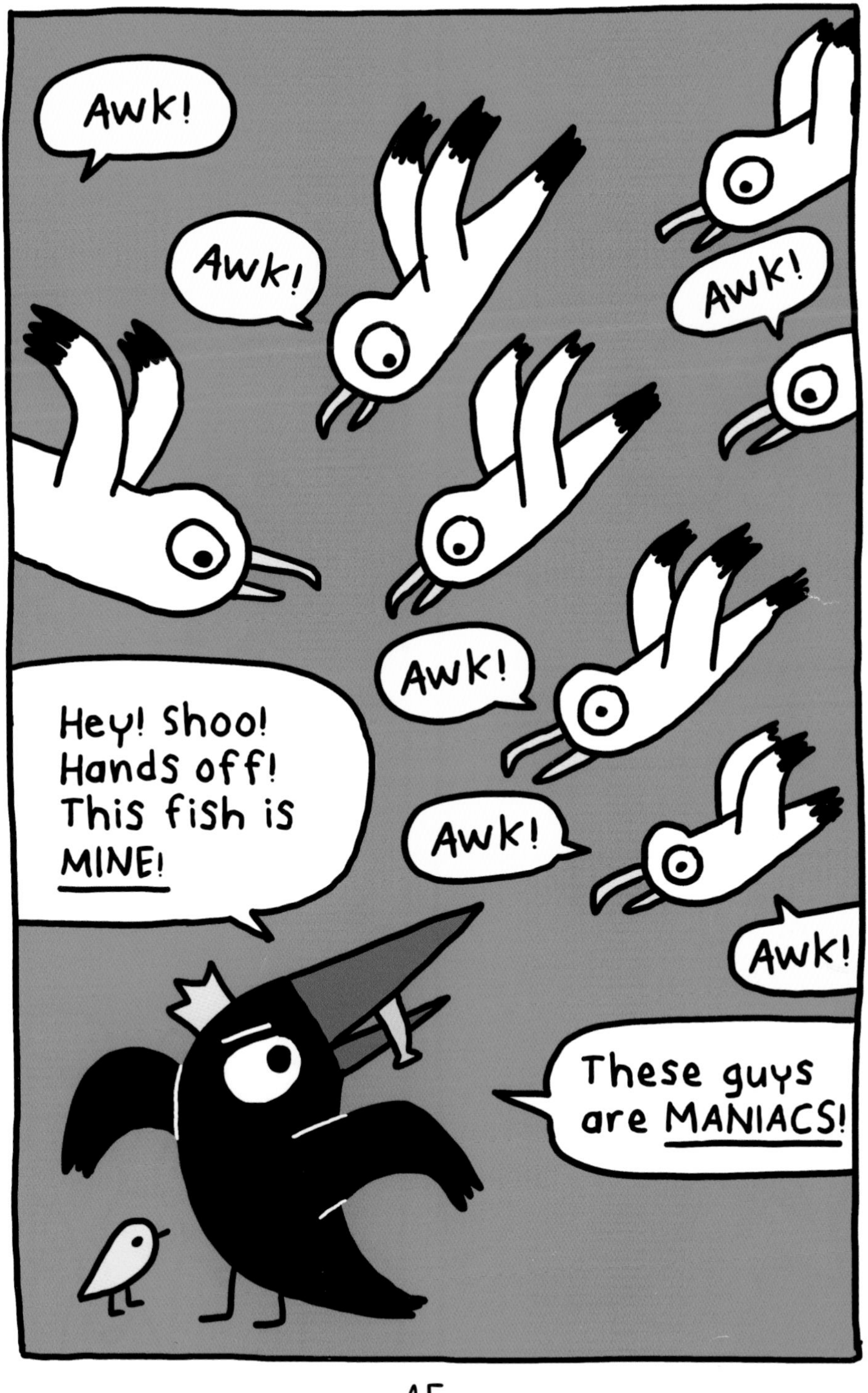
AWK!
AWK!
AWK!
AWK!
Hey! Shoo! Hands off! This fish is MINE!
AWK!
AWK!
These guys are MANIACS!

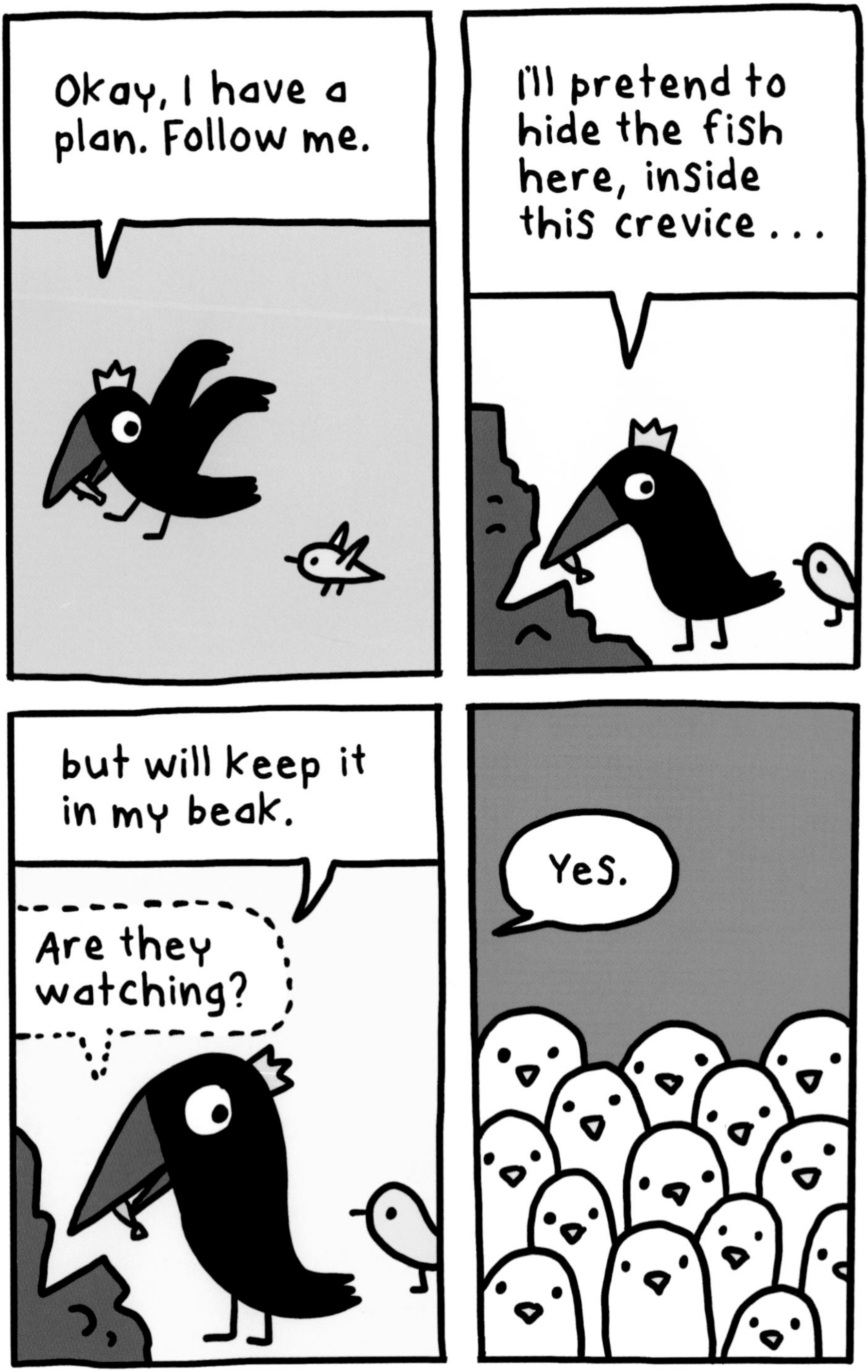
Okay, I have a plan. Follow me.
I'll pretend to hide the fish here, inside this crevice . . .
but will keep it in my beak.
Are they watching?
Yes.

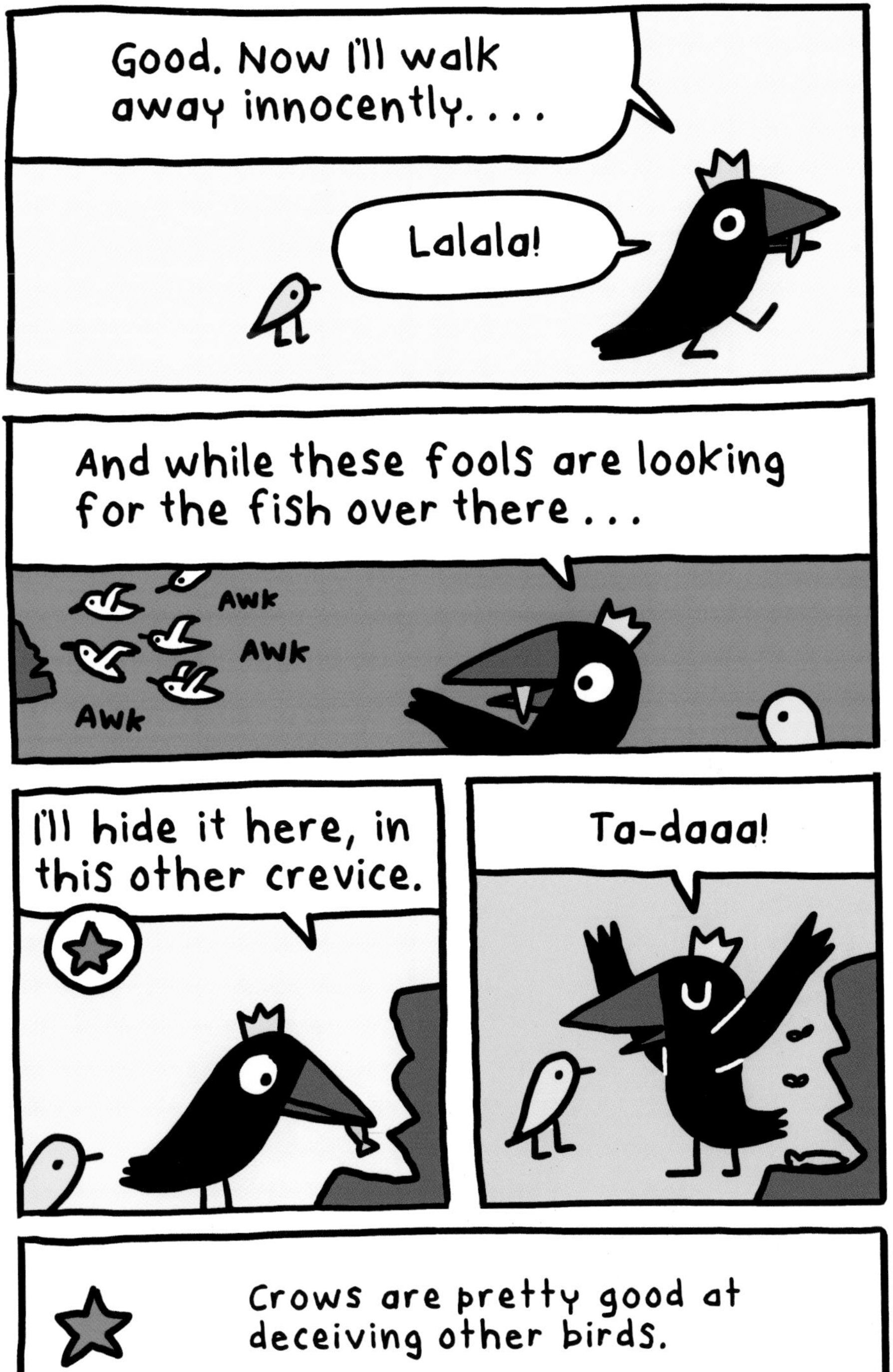
Good. Now I'll walk away innocently. . . .
Lalala!
And while these fools are looking for the fish over there . . .
AWK
AWK
AWK
I'll hide it here, in this other crevice.
Ta-daaa!
Crows are pretty good at deceiving other birds.

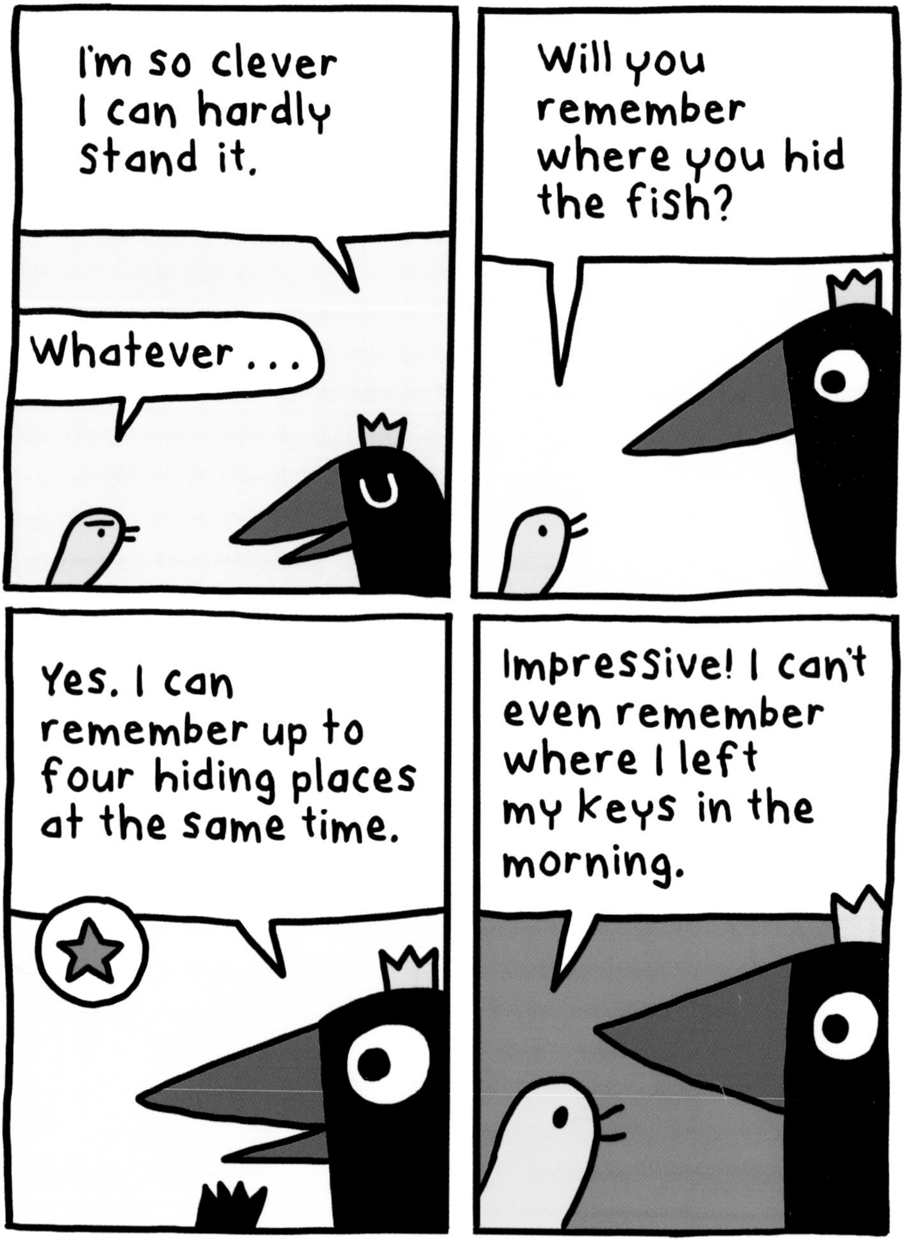
I'm so clever I can hardly stand it.
Whatever . . .
Will you remember where you hid the fish?
Yes. I can remember up to four hiding places at the same time.
Impressive! I can't even remember where I left my keys in the morning.

Crows have an amazing memory!

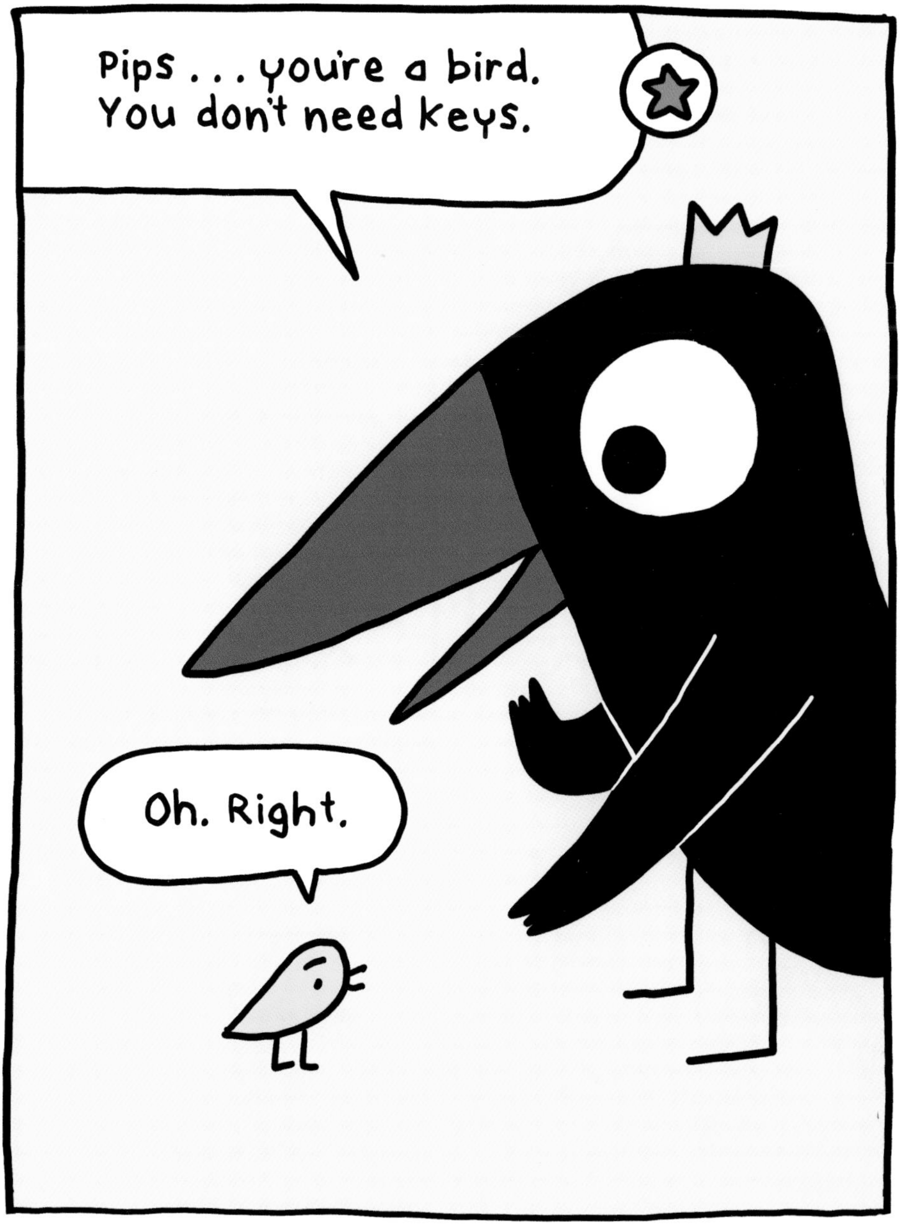
Pips . . . you're a bird. You don't need keys.
Oh. Right.

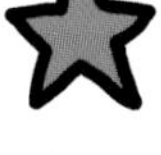
Birds don't need keys.

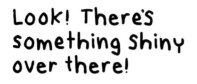

Look! There's something shiny over there!

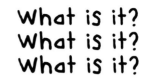

What is it? What is it? What is it?

It's a fork.

Oh my god. It's so beautiful it hurts my eyes.

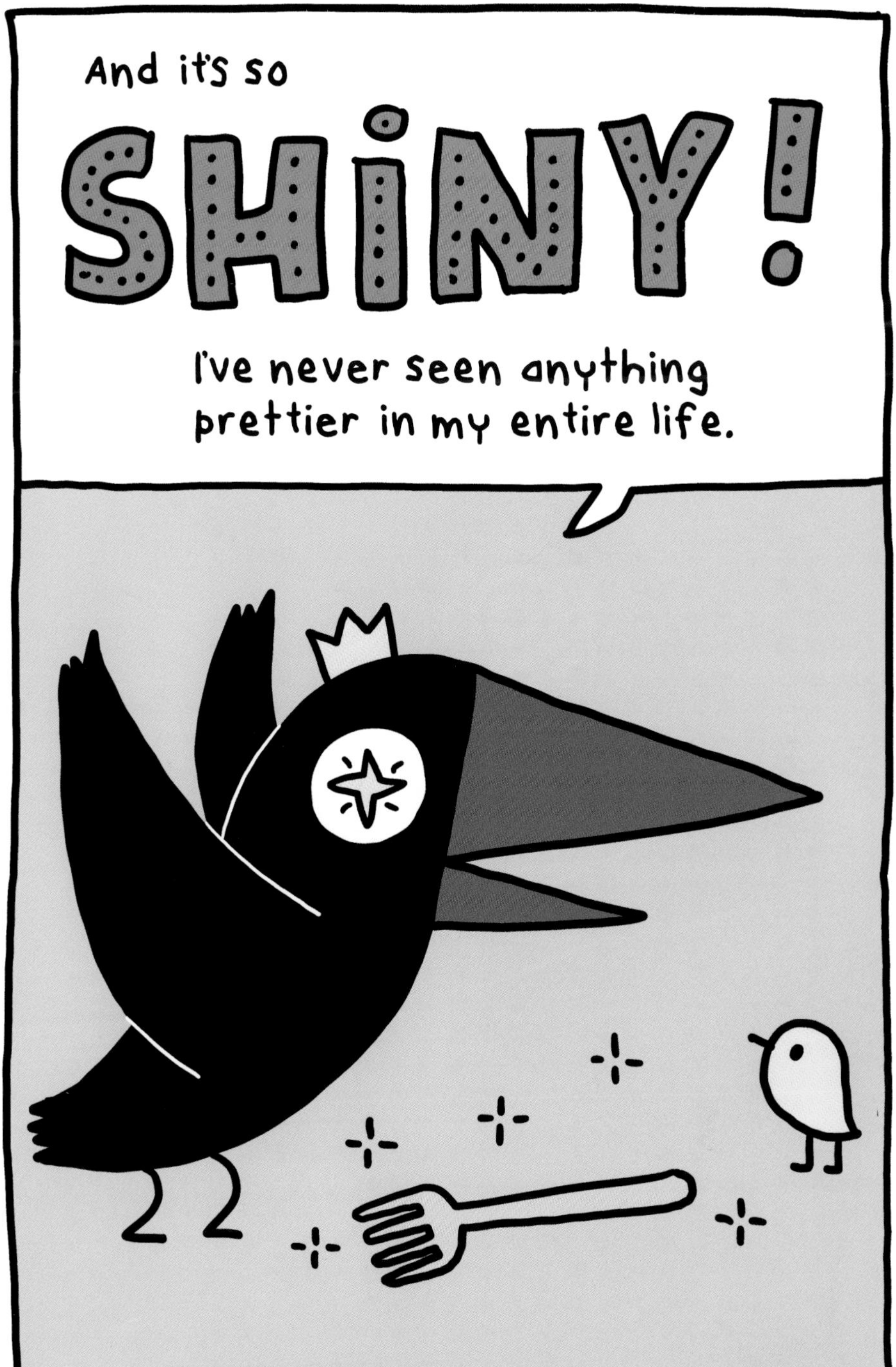
And it's so
SHiNY!
I've never seen anything prettier in my entire life.

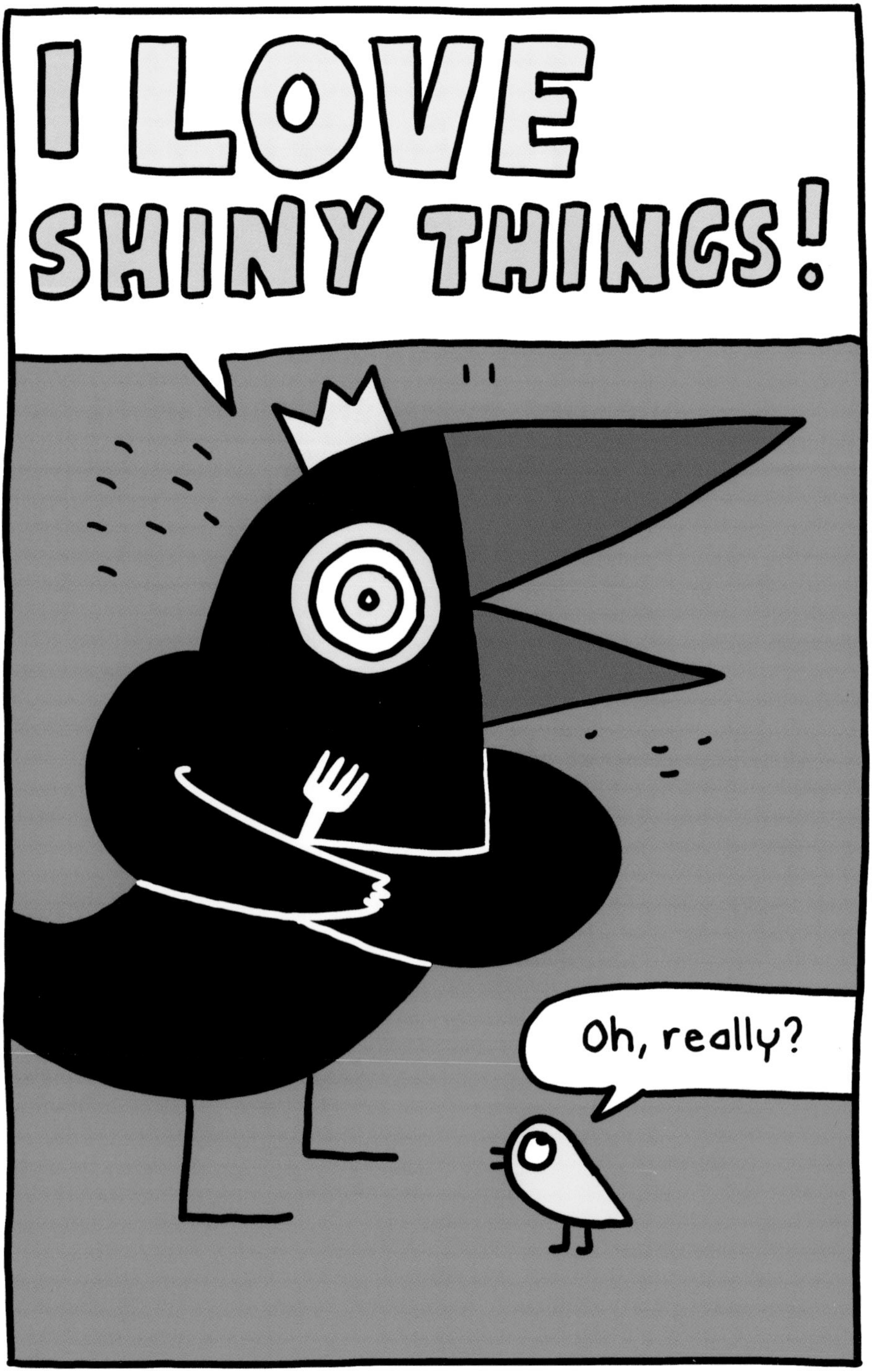
I LOVE SHINY THINGS!
Oh, really?

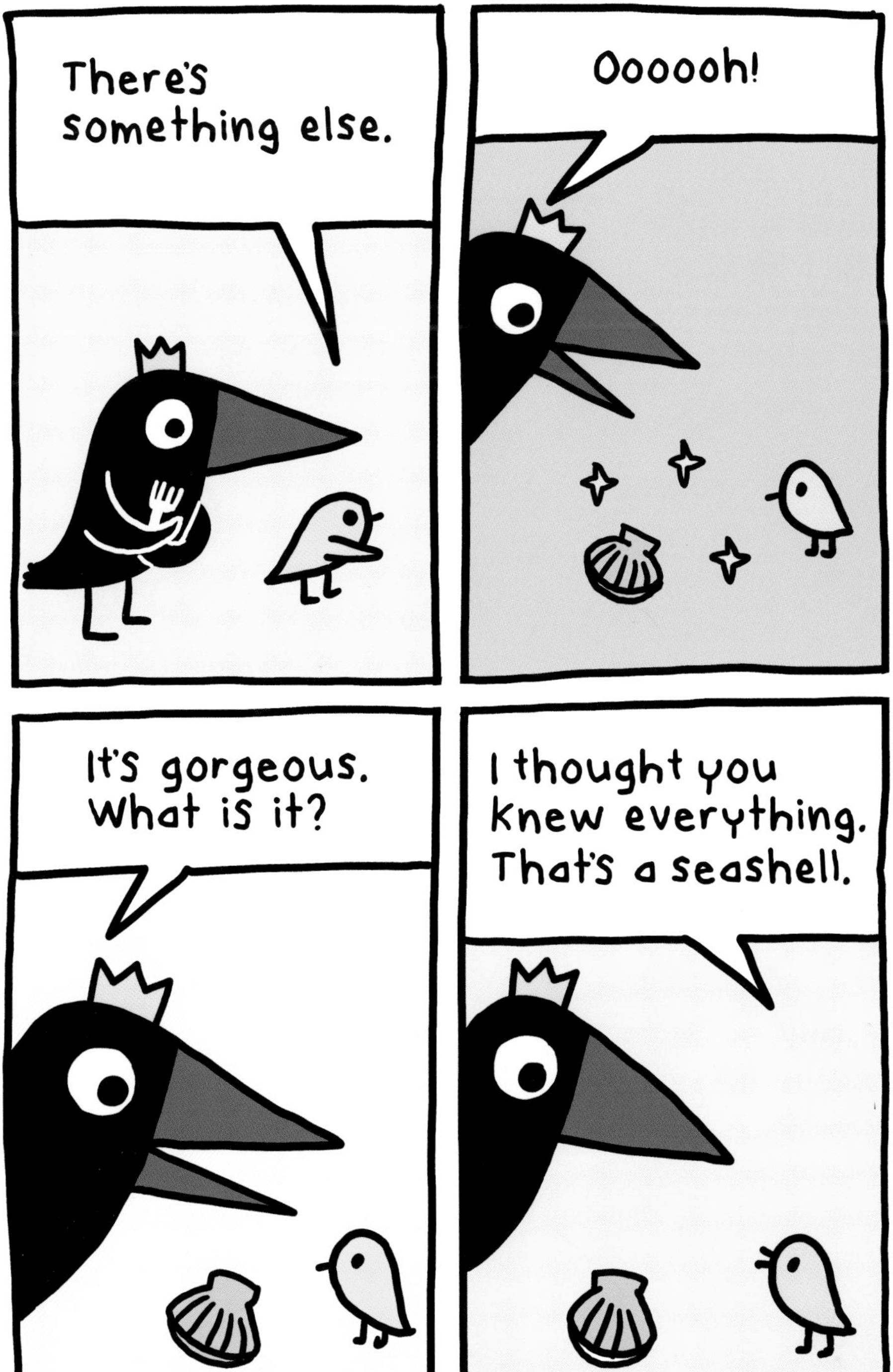
There's something else.
Oooooh!
It's gorgeous. What is it?
I thought you knew everything. That's a seashell.

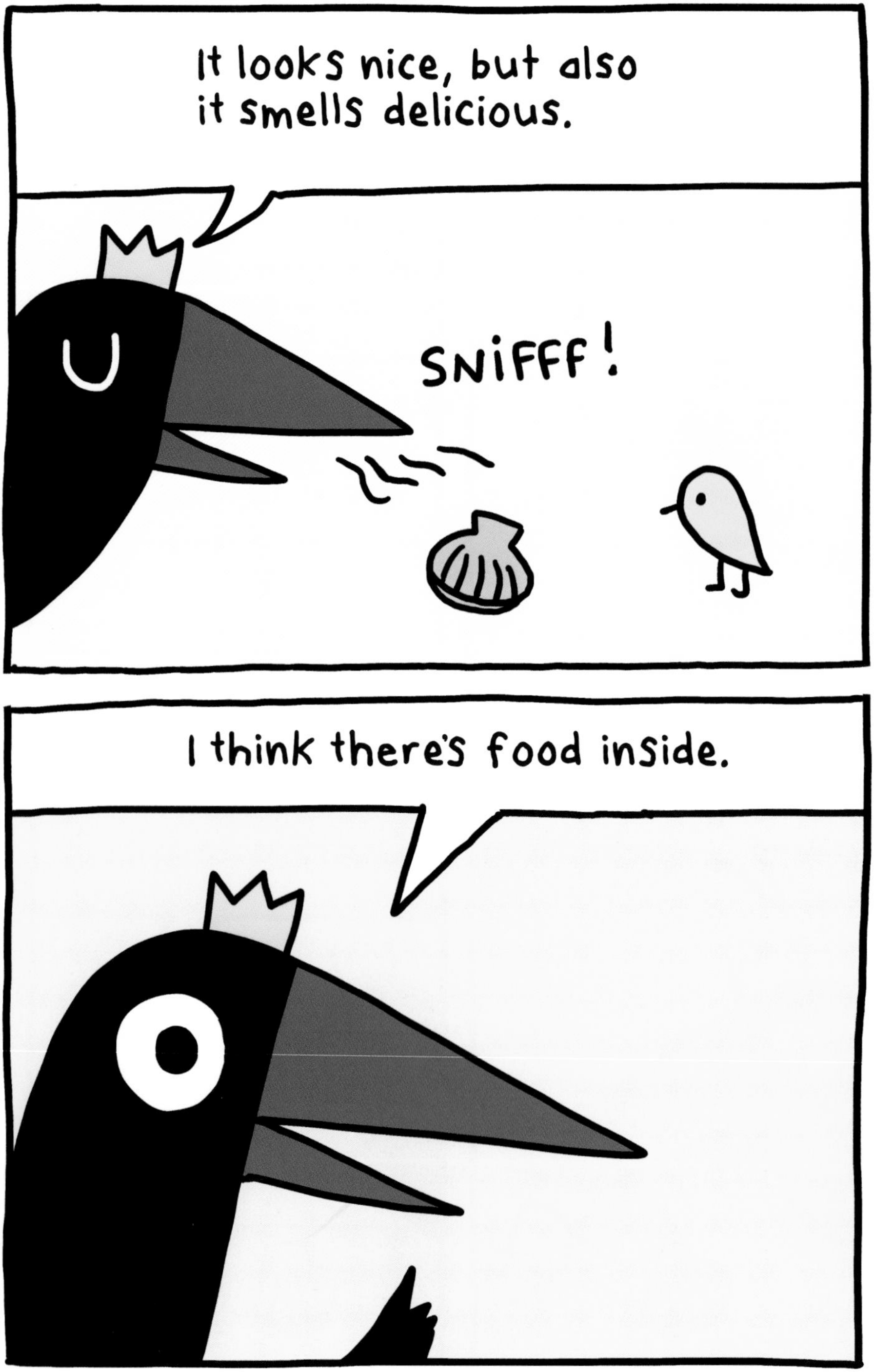
It looks nice, but also
it smells delicious.
SNIFFF!
I think there's food inside.

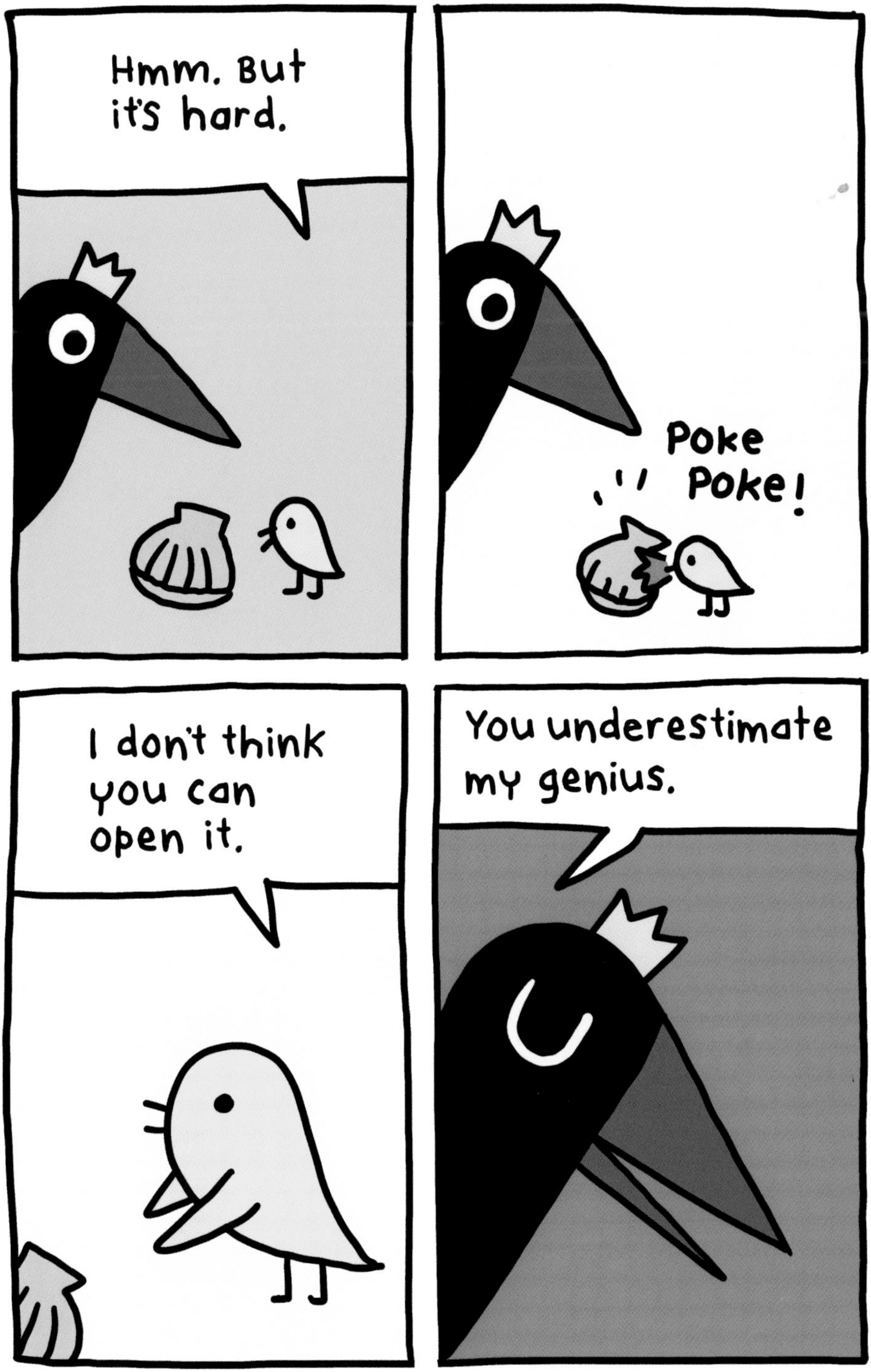
Hmm. But it's hard.
Poke
Poke!
I don't think you can open it.
You underestimate my genius.

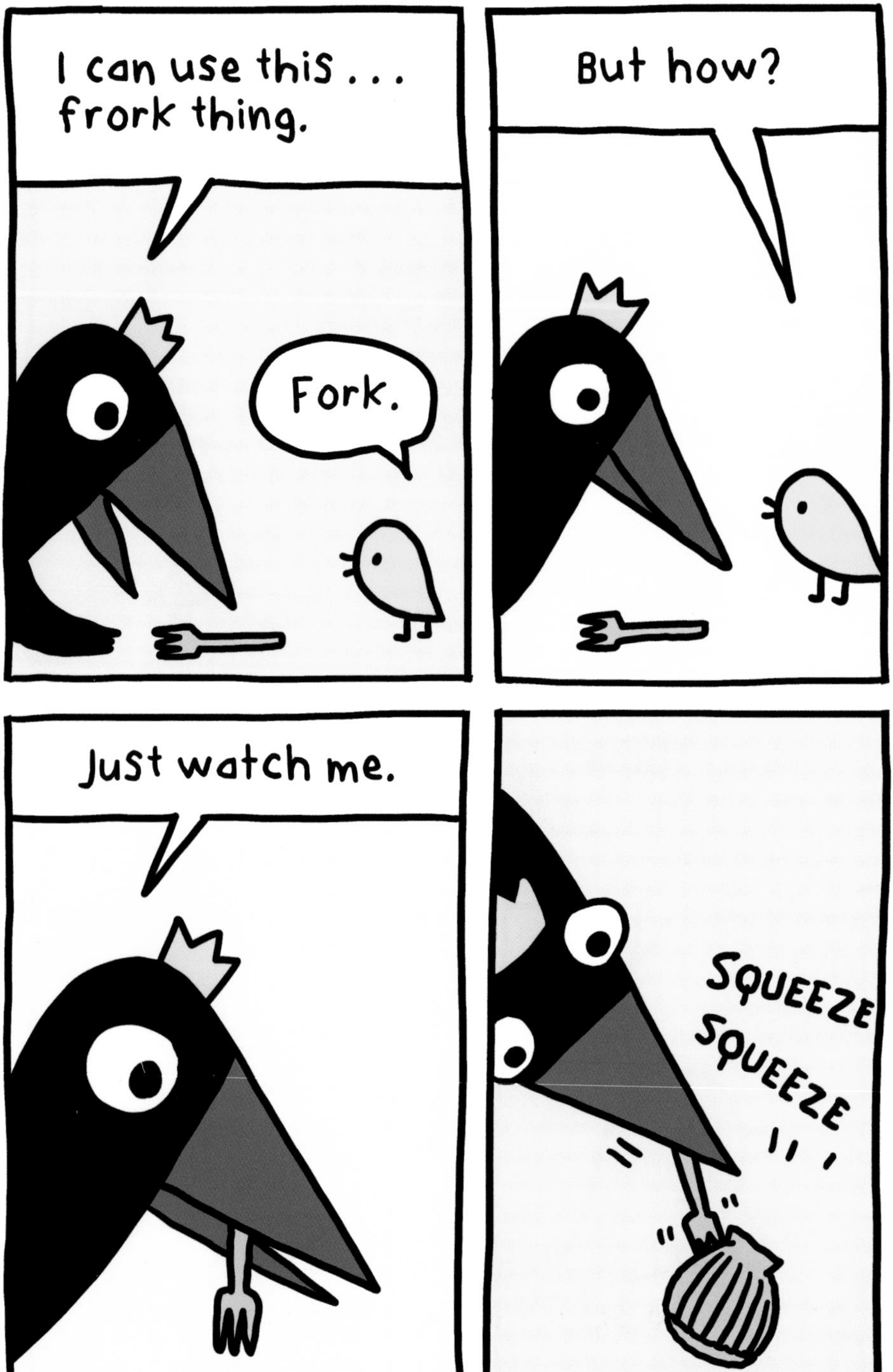
I can use this . . . frork thing.
Fork.
But how?
Just watch me.
SQUEEZE
SQUEEZE

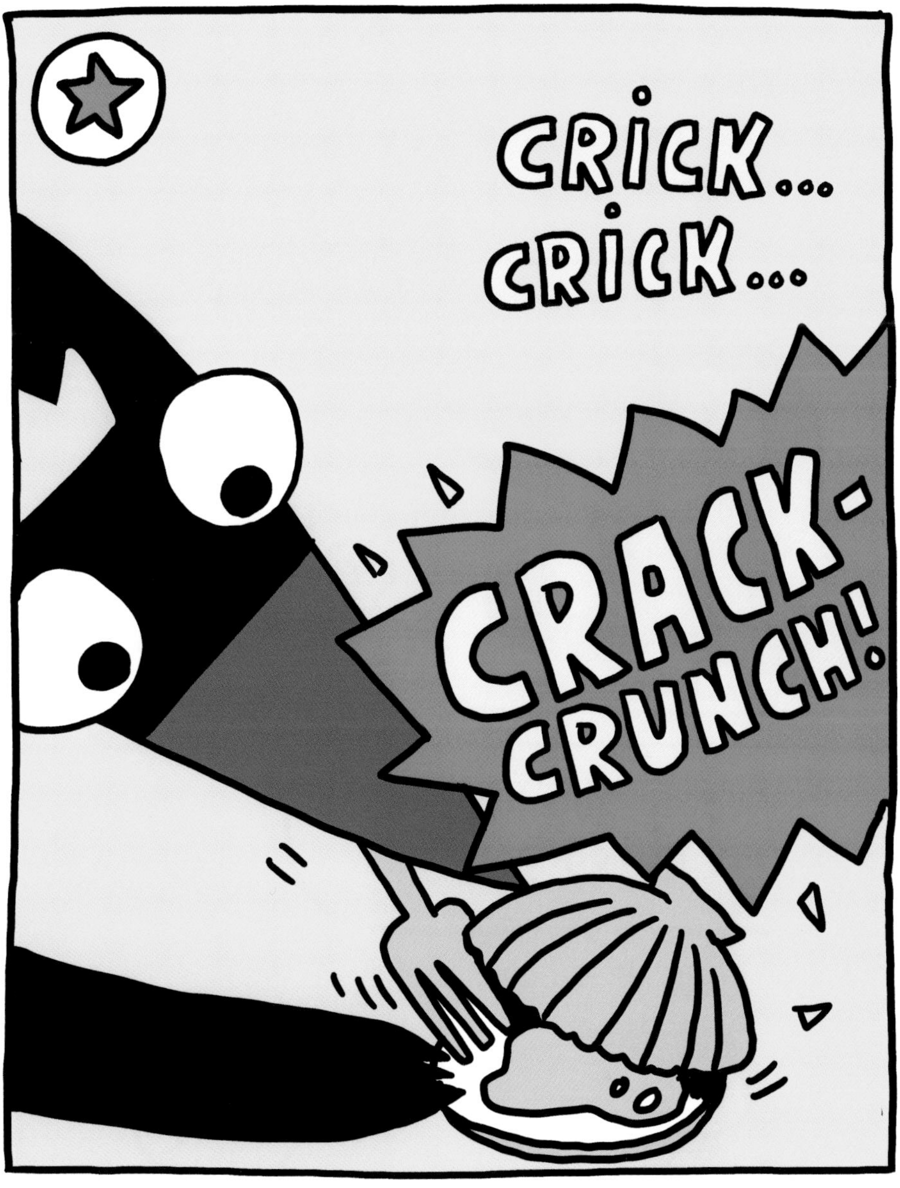
CRICK...
CRICK...
CRACK-
CRUNCH!

Crows can craft and use tools
to access hard-to-reach food.

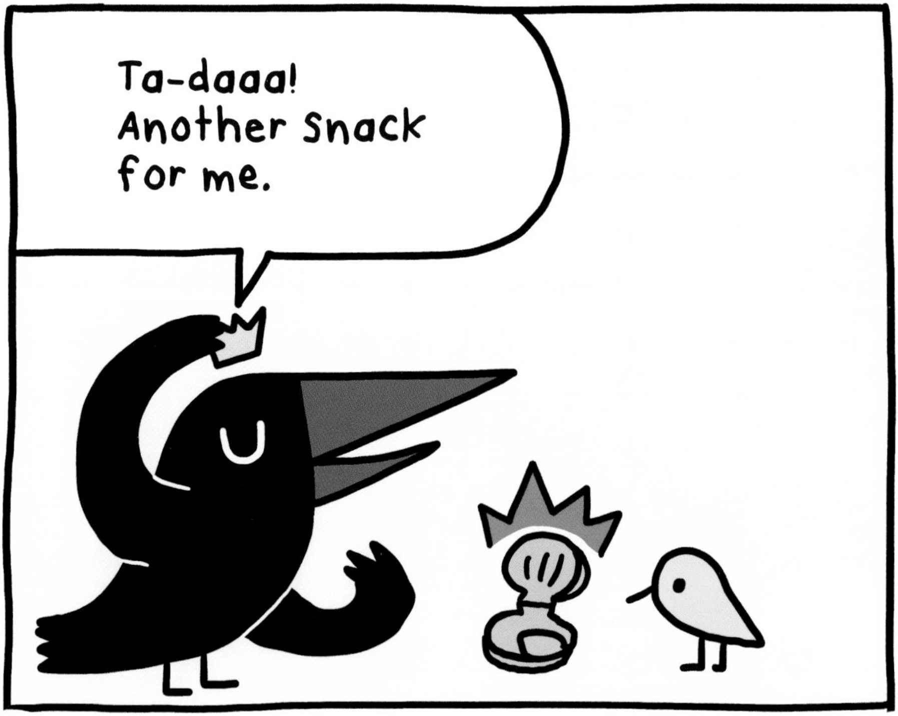
Ta-daaa! Another snack for me.

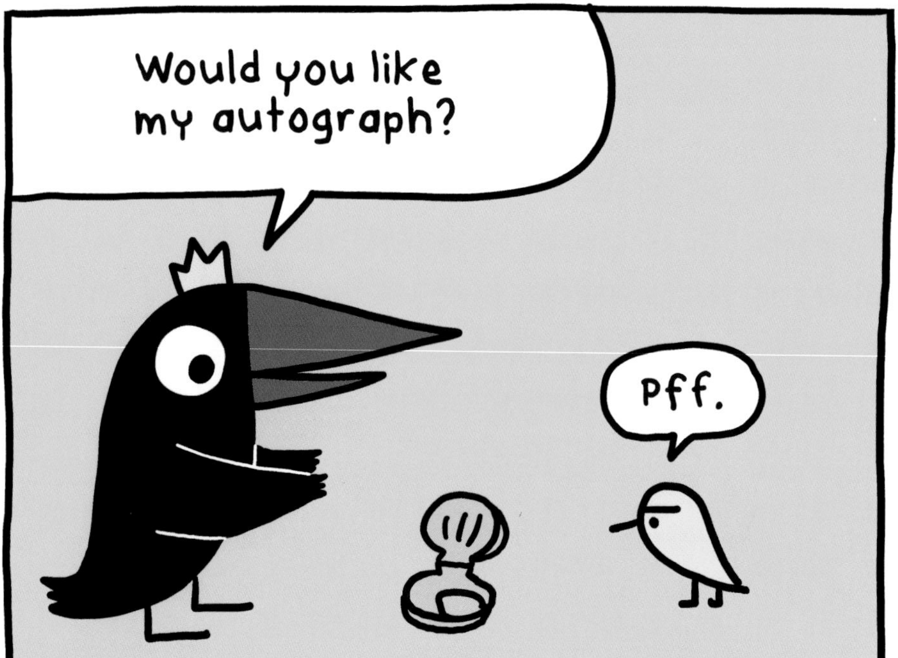
Would you like my autograph?
Pff.

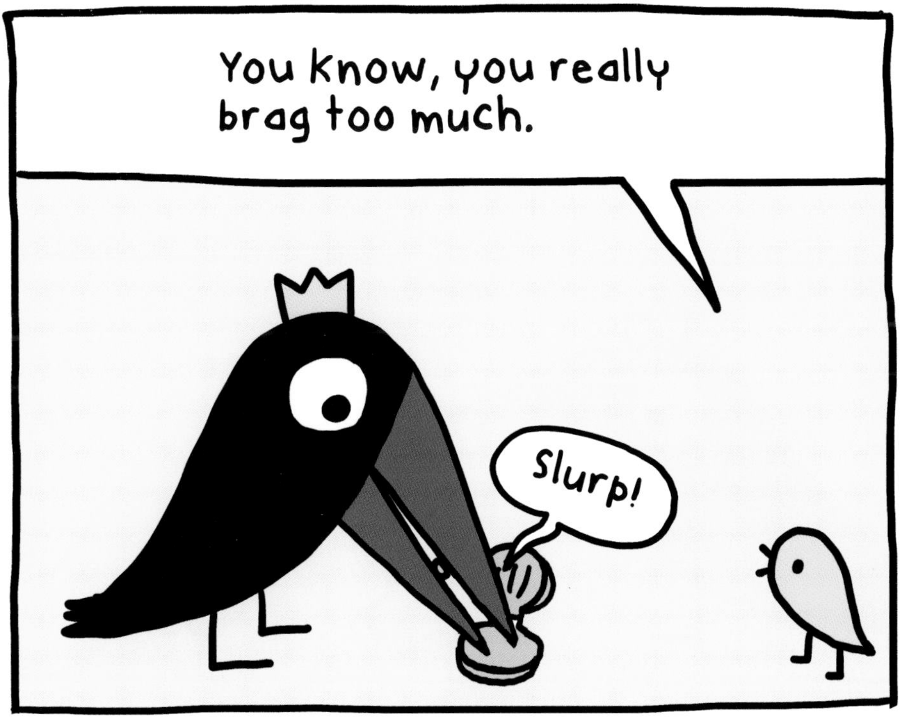
You know, you really brag too much.
Slurp!

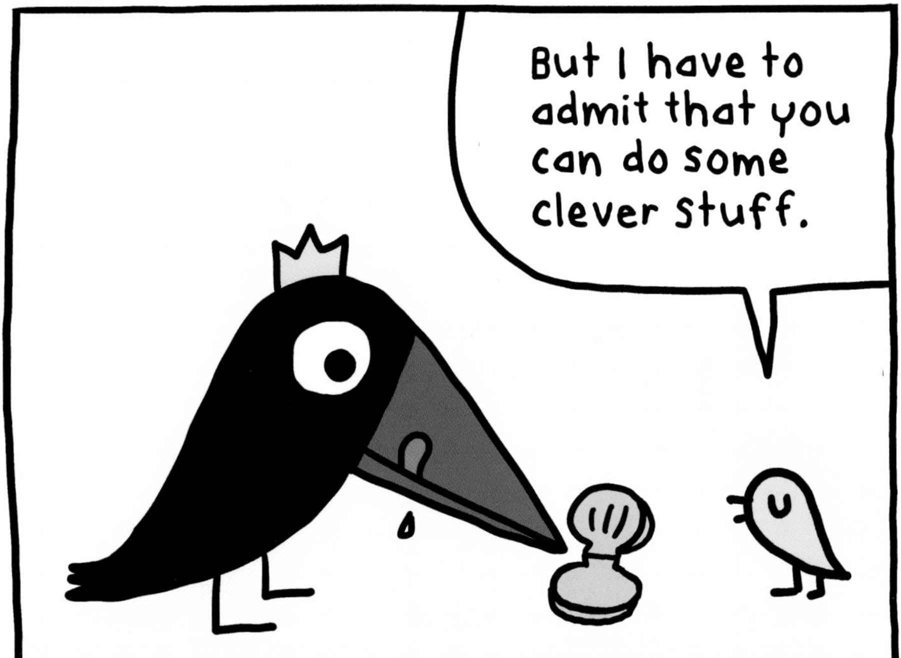
But I have to admit that you can do some clever stuff.

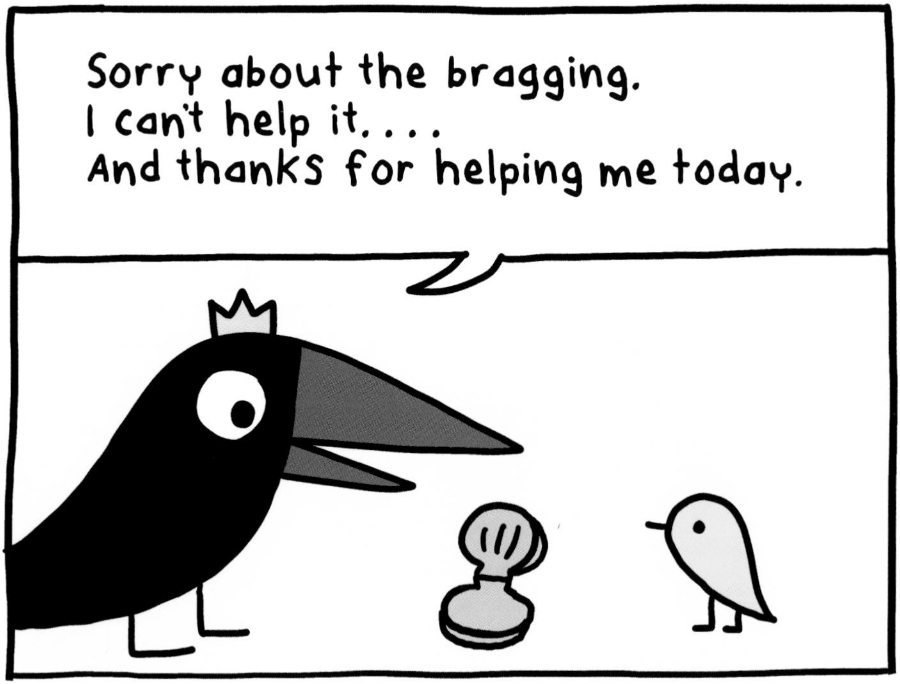
Sorry about the bragging.
I can't help it. . . .
And thanks for helping me today.

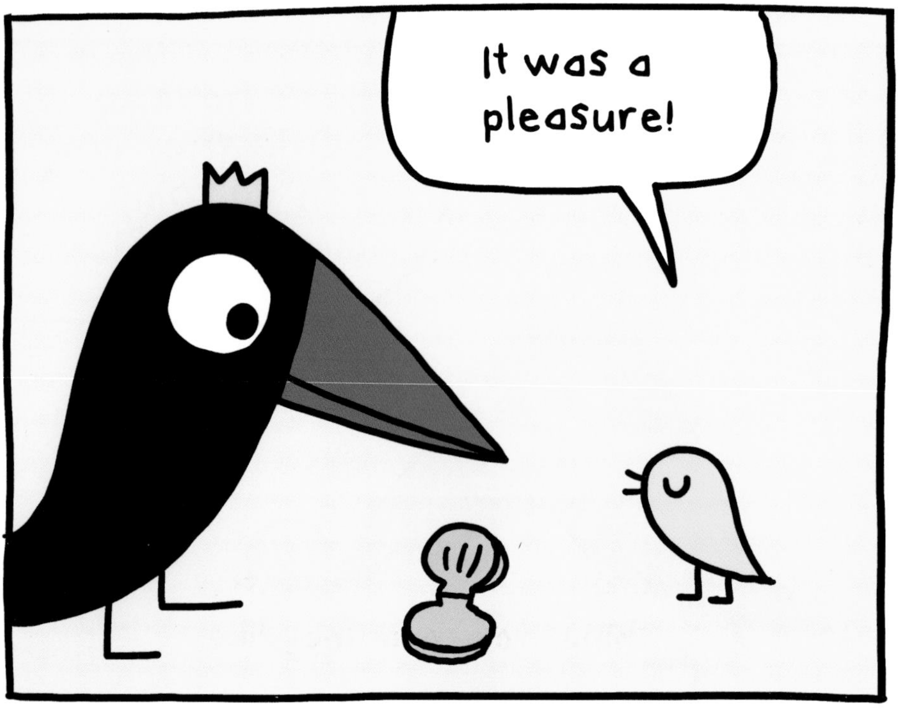
It was a pleasure!

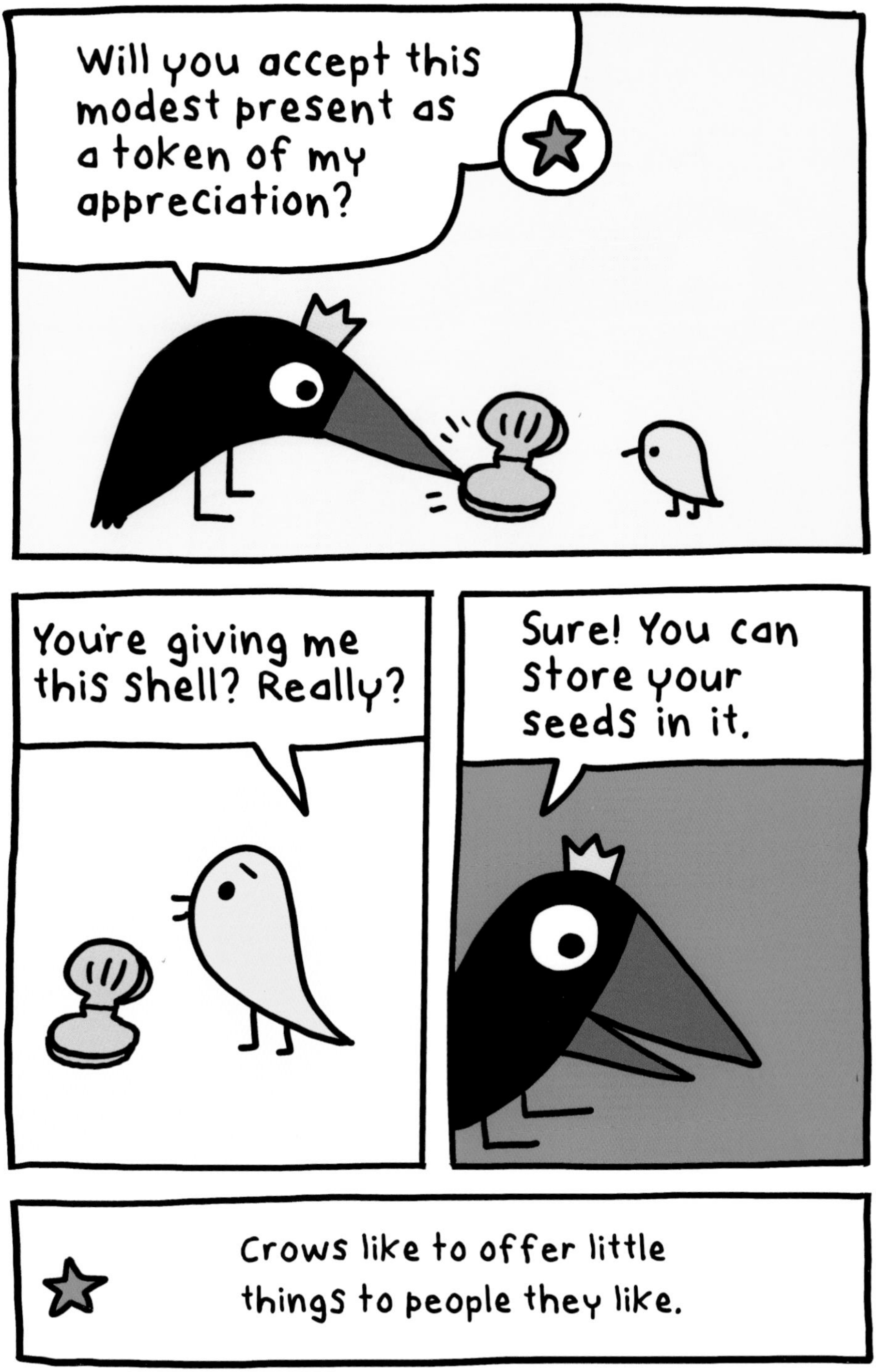
Will you accept this modest present as a token of my appreciation?
You're giving me this shell? Really?
Sure! You can store your seeds in it.
Crows like to offer little things to people they like.

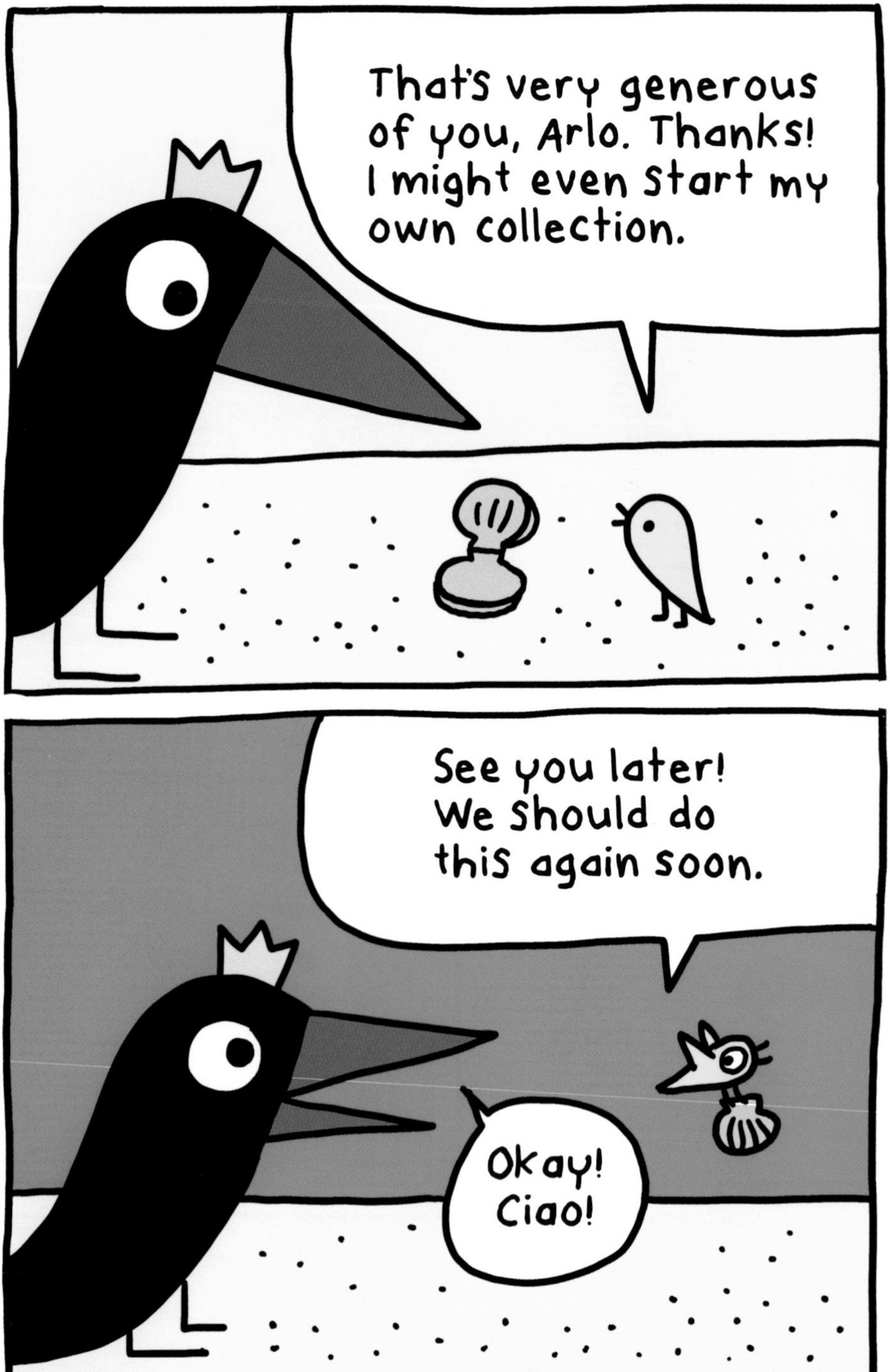
That's very generous of you, Arlo. Thanks! I might even start my own collection.
See you later! We should do this again soon.
Okay! Ciao!

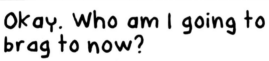

Okay. Who am I going to brag to now?

## THE END

STAY TUNED FOR
MORE ADVENTURES OF . . .

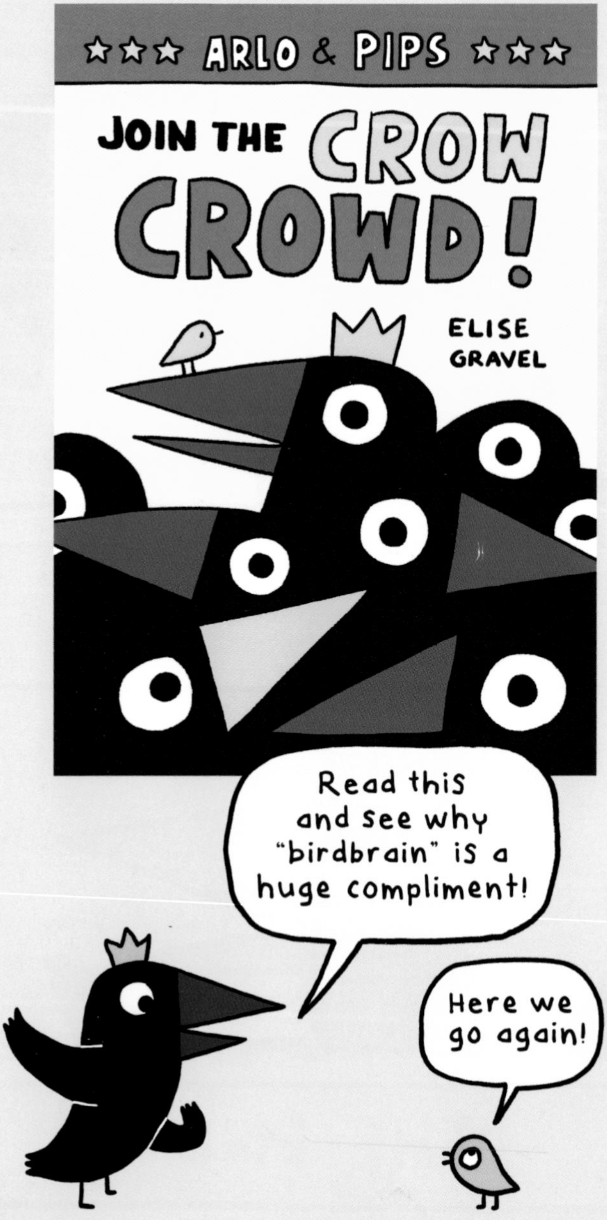
ARLO & PIPS
JOIN THE CROW CROWD!
ELISE GRAVEL
Read this and see why "birdbrain" is a huge compliment!
Here we go again!

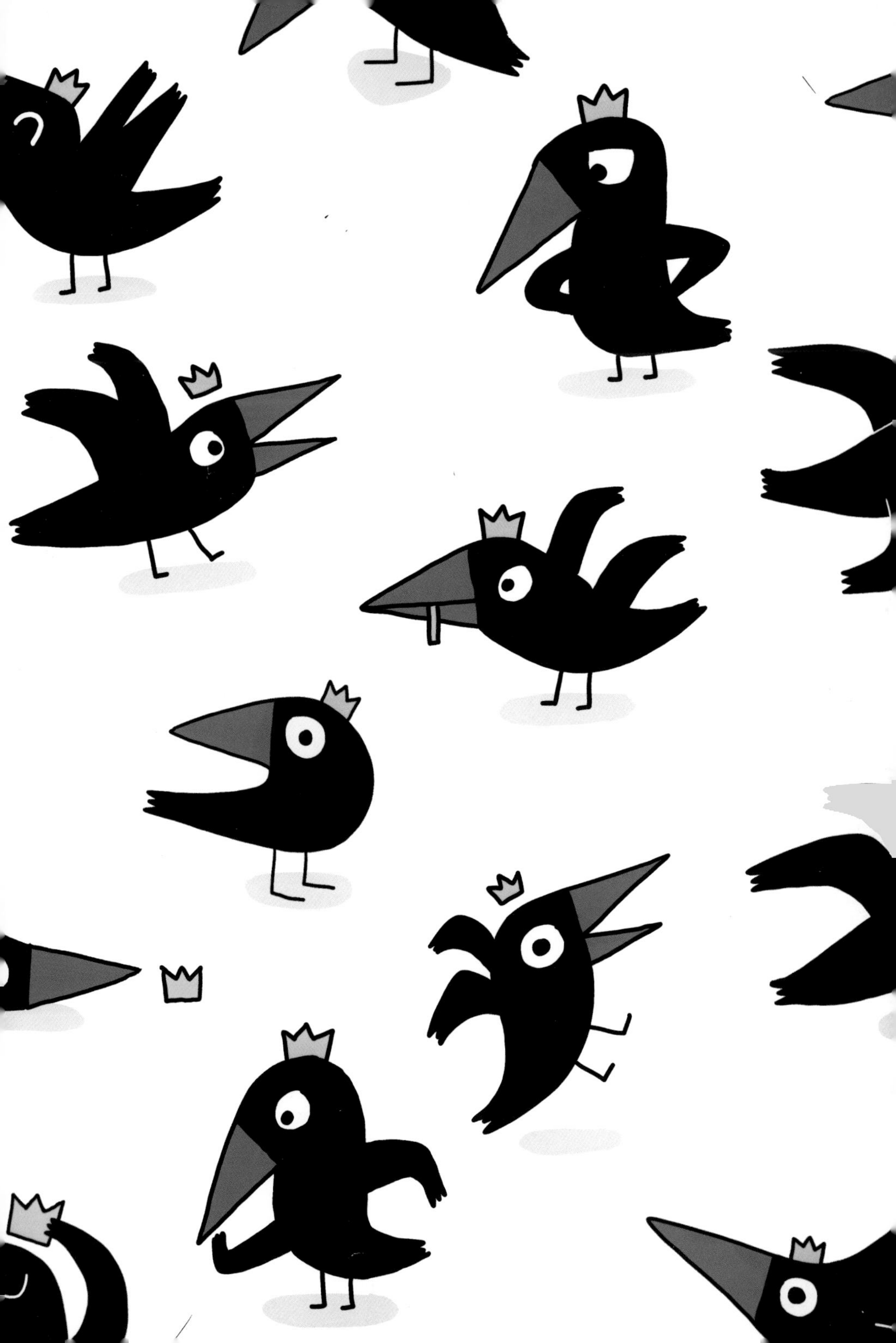

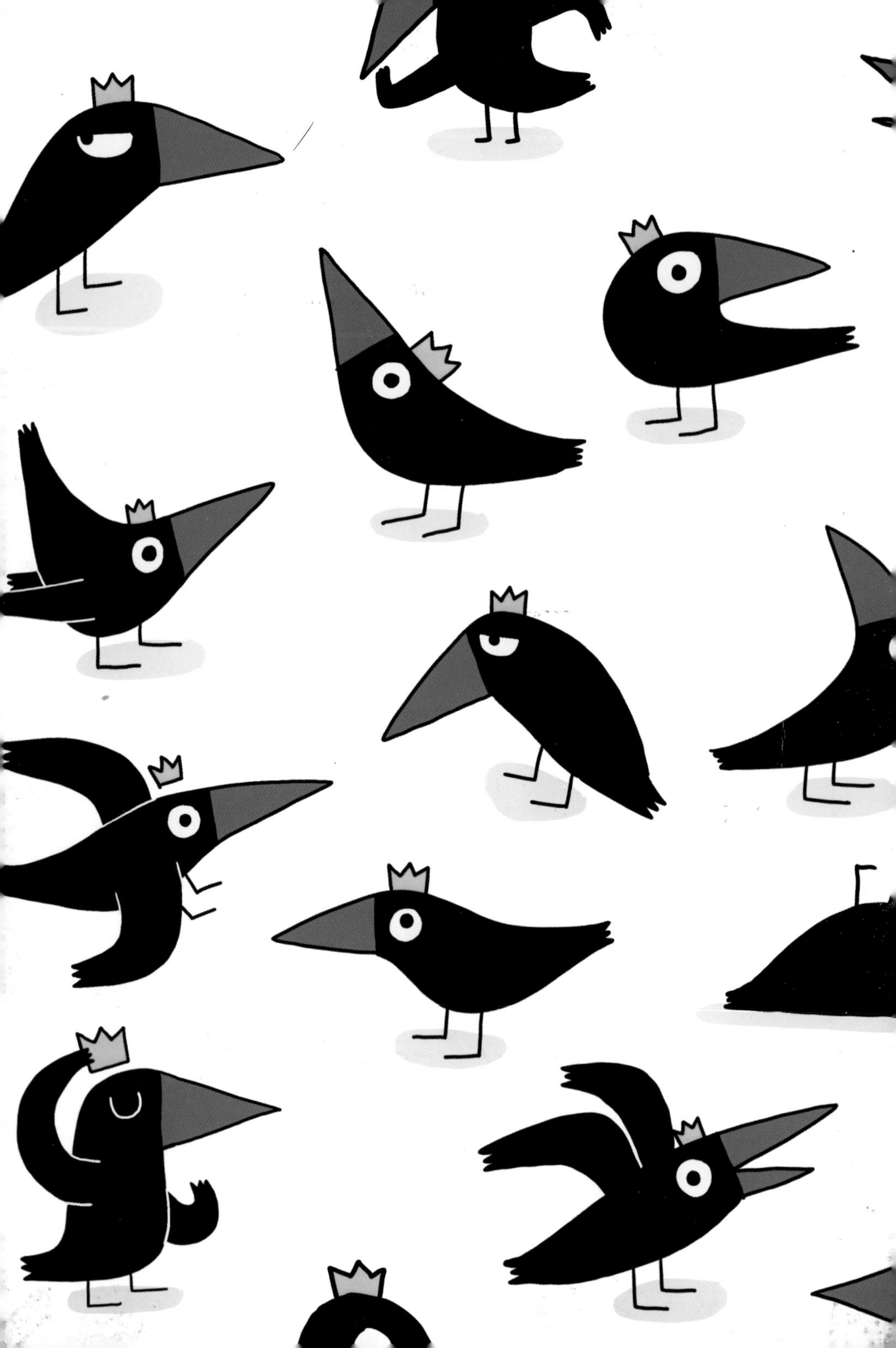